Isolt's

Enchantment

Daughter of Light

A Prequel

A Young Adult Fantasy Trilogy by

Heidi Garrett

Isolt's Enchantment by Heidi Garrett

Half-Faerie Publishing

Copyright © 2017 by Heidi Garrett

Find out more about Heidi Garrett at

www.heidigwrites.blogspot.com

Cover Art by JWB

Editing by Vince Dickinson

ISBN: 978-0-9907691-1-8

For

Carol Ann Baker

Contents

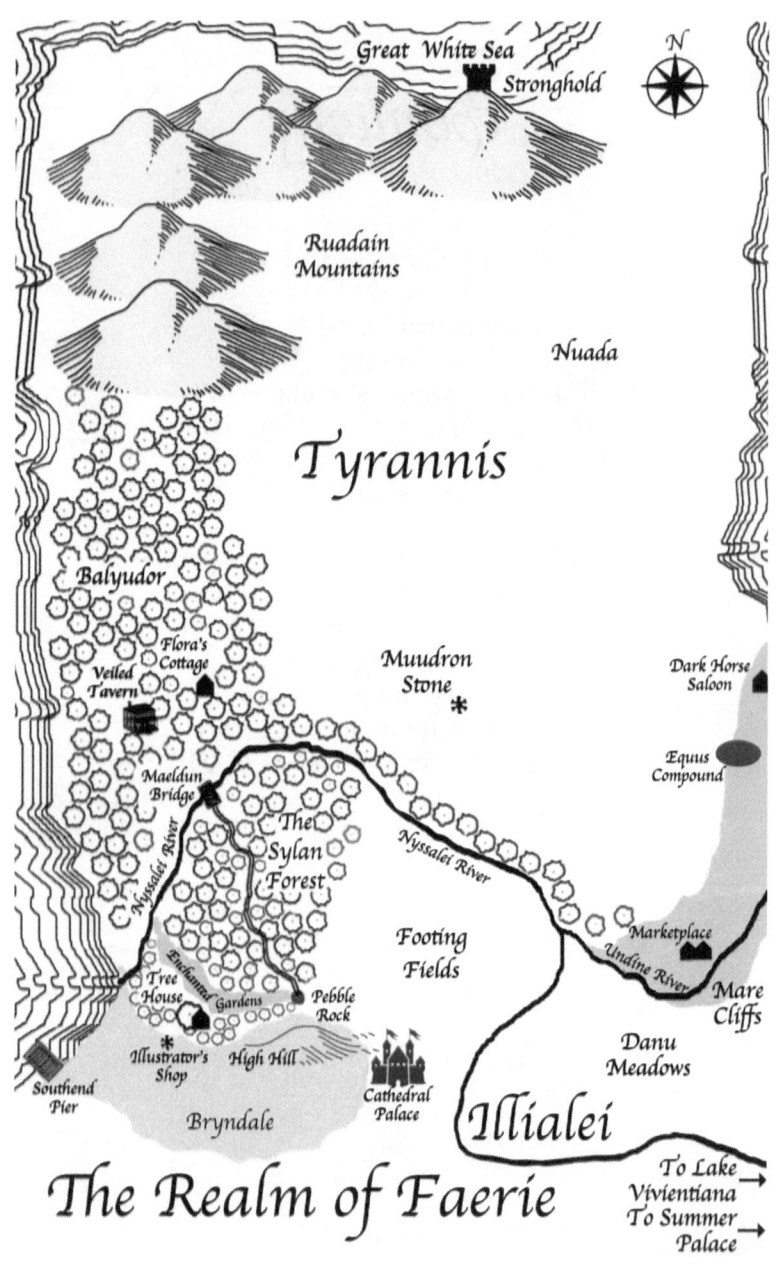

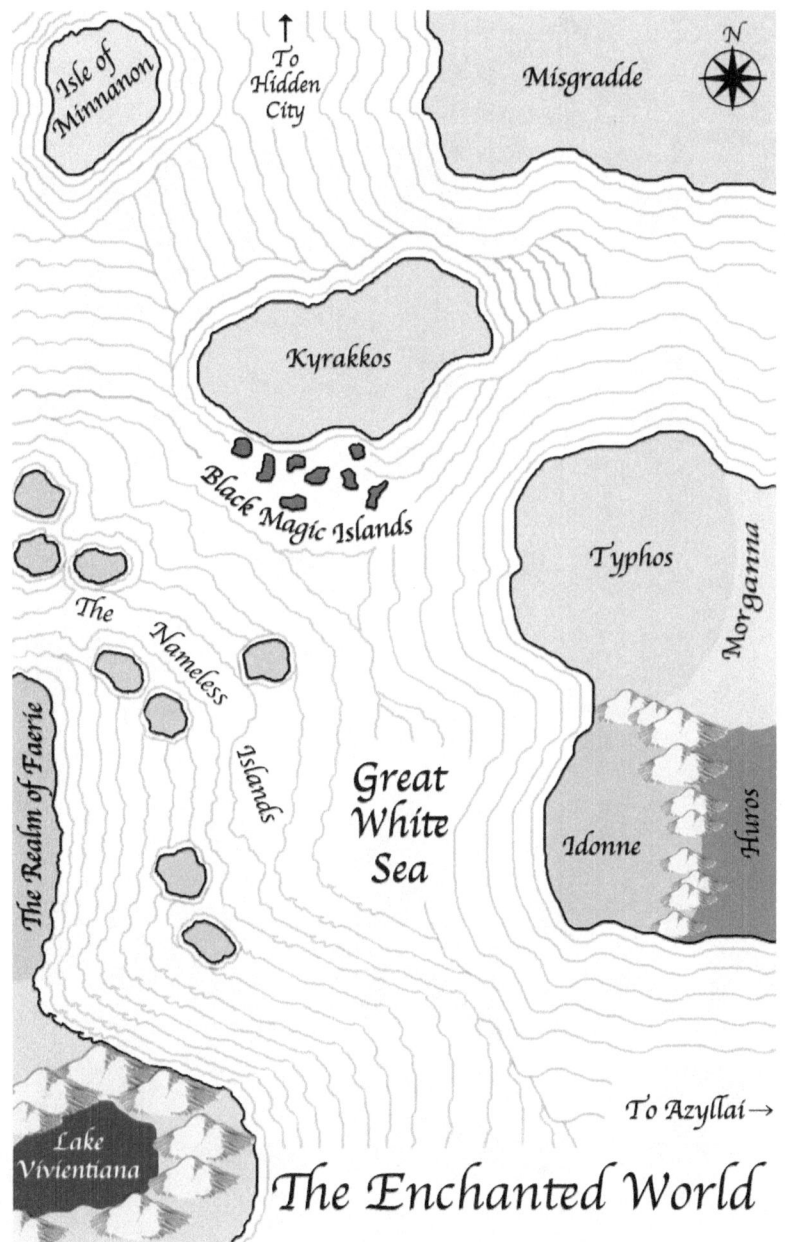

The Enchanted World

The Stargazer

The maned visage roared in Celeste's mind. Etched on a lambent gold shell, harvested from the depths of the Great White Sea, its regal quality drew the mortal woman's hand. Above all the exquisite rattles on display, the lion's tawny head resonated most deeply with the hopes she held for her child.

She lifted it from the cloth-covered surface with trembling fingers. Pinhead-sized jewels embellished the detailed engraving. It wasn't necessary to inquire the price to know the toy was more than she'd intended to spend. She returned the rattle to its resting place among the others. Her gaze lingered over the pearlesque mermaid swishing her tail fin, a pair of rose-tinted wings that made Celeste think first of a butterfly but were more likely modeled after a faerie, and a satiny blue flower whose long, slim

1

petals reminded her of a lily.

The shopkeeper approached. "Is this your first?"

"Mmm," Celeste murmured.

"A boy or a girl?"

"A boy."

He selected a gleaming gold-orange ball and gave it a good shake. "The sun."

Celeste smiled but didn't take the rattle. She pressed her knuckles against her mouth and lowered her eyes.

"But it won't do, if it doesn't appeal to his mother." He watched her face as his hand hovered over each design. When he reached the lion head, it was impossible to quench the light in her eyes. "The lion, then. Dignity, loyalty, courage. It's an excellent choice for a boy."

"I fear I can't afford it," Celeste admitted.

The shopkeeper crossed his arms as they studied one another. "Perhaps we could agree to a fair price."

Celeste's reserve loosened as she considered his offer. If she spent her last piece of gold on this rattle, she would still have enough silver to pay for her room and board at the temple, and a few pieces of copper for incidentals. But she'd have none left to travel back across the mountains—or anywhere else—after the baby was born. If she was honest with herself, she had no intention of leaving Idonne. The boy needed to be close to his father. Whether or not he claimed his son. Celeste pushed the weight of her dark hair away from her face. She'd never dreamed this for her future, and yet, here she was; pregnant, and falling deeply in love with the child growing in her belly.

She named her price.

"That is a generous offer from one so far from home and with so little to spare," the shopkeeper observed.

Celeste shrugged. It no longer surprised her when someone in the enchanted world read her correctly, and the Idonnai were as good as any. The boy's father had exploited her fascination for esoteric knowledge to bed her. At least it had made for intriguing pillow talk. And the child in her womb would be intelligent. But she wasn't completely devoid of perceptive skills herself. She responded, "We both know you made that rattle for my son."

The shopkeeper's narrow face cracked into a wide grin. Many of these artisans enjoyed a lively negotiation more than mounds of gold. Celeste returned his smile. She would talk until the sun set if it meant she could make a gift of the lion head rattle to her newborn son.

Celeste startled awake, the palm of her hand compressed against her chest as if to stop her heart from bursting from its confines. Damp strands of hair plastered her temples. Twisted sheets trapped her legs in belligerent knots. She kicked away the taut cloth, springing from the modest cot as if it seared her flesh.

It was not yet dawn, the room's single window a grey square framed by black-shadowed wall. She stretched onto her tiptoes. Allowing the sea breeze to caress her fevered cheeks, she gulped in salty air.

With life stirring in her belly, she felt invincible. And yet, her dreams warned her of some harsh fate. She dropped her heels to the floor and paced. Her bold resolve to face Anton wavered. The priest had never told her he loved her. Their trysts had been few. She could count them on one hand—with fingers to spare.

Celeste splashed tepid water on her cheeks and tied her hair into a loose knot. Wrapped in her sea-blue cloak, she left her room. The long walk to the market would clear her head.

Before she'd walked too far, the first song of the day reached Celeste's ears. She paused. Each dawn and sunset, the priestesses of the Temple of Delphinus lined up on the temple steps to worship a world of imagined perfection with their hymns. She'd always found the music deeply moving. A short distance from the side of the road was a rocky ledge. Celeste reached out to steady herself against it—and to listen. Her thoughts floated higher and higher. By the time the performance ended, she was settled comfortably on the shelf of rock, dreaming a bright future for herself and her son. A fantasy perhaps, but the reverie swished the remnants of her nightmare aside and energized her.

She marched off to the market with renewed determination.

Celeste observed the old woman through the window of her empty shop. There was nothing unusual about her. She had the same long face and wore the same sand-colored garb as all the Idonnai. When the stargazer craned her head in Celeste's direction, the mortal woman shrank away from the window. With her back pressed against the white stucco wall of the market, she tried to imagine what the woman could tell her that she didn't already know.

Sandals shuffled in her direction. A kindly face peered from the shop's arch. "Come in, my dear."

Celeste shook her head at her distrust. This woman was not some mortal shyster who would take her money and offer a bland fortune of a tall, dark stranger and wealth in her future. She was a stargazer. They sighted specific, seemingly innocuous details that could alter a destiny. Celeste straightened her shoulders and entered the shop.

The stargazer indicated a plain chair at a plain table. "Sit, my dear."

Celeste made no effort to hide her swelling belly as she lowered her bulk awkwardly into the chair. The days of hiding her pregnancy in the folds of her cloak were long past.

The stargazer slid an oblong mirror onto the table before she sat across from Celeste. She offered her hands, palms up. "Place your hands in mine." The old woman gazed into the mirror's surface and began to hum. It wasn't a musical sound, more like the buzzing of bees. The mirror darkened and, as in the night sky, stars appeared. The stargazer concentrated on the oracle.

She gave her client's hands a final squeeze before releasing them. "I'm sorry, my dear. The news is mixed."

Celeste stared down at the array of blinking lights, meaningless to her.

"Your boy will be healthy. He will live to be strong, not only in body, but also in mind." The old woman leaned forward and pressed her palm against Celeste's breastbone.

The mortal woman melted into the gesture, as if life itself flowed from the stargazer's palm.

"And his heart will be unwavering."

Tears formed in Celeste's eyes. When she'd discovered she carried a boy, conflicting feelings had possessed her. Beginning with her father, her every relationship with a male had been a disaster. To know that her son would grow into a decent man was worth the stargazer's fee. She embraced the news and the burden it lifted.

"But there will be complications with the boy's father."

Celeste sucked in a breath. She pushed away the heavy curl that fell against her cheek. "He doesn't know yet. I was going to tell him today."

The stargazer lifted her eyes to meet her client's gaze. "If you go to him now, he'll deny the child is his."

"Then, when?"

"After the child is born. Can you wait that long?"

"I have a room at the Temple of Delphinus. The priestesses are gracious and respect my privacy. My little room has a window facing north. The coastal breezes and ocean's constant lullaby calms me. And every time I hear the choir sing, it elevates my spirit. I've already been assigned a midwife who seems proficient. I suppose I have no reason to leave before the baby's born."

"Good, good," the stargazer encouraged.

"But last night, my dreams were dark! That's why I came here

7

rather than making the trip to meet with the boy's father. I'm afraid he might take the child from me."

"That is not the threat that hangs over you."

Celeste's heart lurched. "What is?"

"A mortal woman has journeyed alone to bear a child in Idonne," the old woman observed. "I need no oracle to tell me the boy's father is a member of the Order of the Idonnai."

Celeste made no effort to refute the woman's claim.

"There is a shadow over the boy's father," the stargazer said. "And yet, to fulfill his destiny, the boy must know him."

The room shrank around Celeste. She had an impulse to seize the oracle, to smash it, to silence the news that troubled her more than her own imaginings.

"But there are some things you can do," the stargazer continued.

"Anything," Celeste said. "I'll do anything to protect my child and safeguard his future."

"What I tell you may seem simple, trivial perhaps. But please, do as I say."

A riot of nausea and lightheadedness cooled Celeste's body. Why had she come here? What if she couldn't follow the stargazer's instructions?

"Purchase a reed basket."

Her galloping heart slowed down.

"Line it with a warm blanket."

Celeste nodded. She could do these things.

"When you experience your first contraction, tuck the child's gift inside."

Within the folds of her cloak, Celeste gripped the rattle's twined handle. She had no need to ask how the woman knew of the fine present she'd bought for her son.

"Keep the basket close during the birth." The stargazer's eyes drifted. "It will become clear what to do with these things when the time comes."

❖ ❖ ❖

Celeste's fingers curled through the golden lacework that bound the private world of the Order of the Idonnai.

From the corner of her eye, she watched the priests distribute alms to the beggars lined up outside the citadel gate. She maintained a careful distance. Although she had no need for charity, curiosity impelled her to join the crowd that waited for food and assistance each morning. The gathered poor would be dispersed before the sun reached its apex in the sky. The Idonnic priests discouraged loitering.

Celeste would leave with them.

A young priest, moving down the row of paupers, stopped beside her with a wooden bowl filled to the rim with steaming porridge and roots.

Although she wasn't hungry, Celeste almost accepted the food —to extend the day's visit. It would be one of her last for awhile; her time was close. "I'm only here to admire the citadel's golden gates." She'd arranged the blue cloak to shadow her dark hair and unusual green eyes.

Despite her attempt to draw attention away from her appearance, the priest studied her face. "You're not from Idonne."

Celeste lowered her eyes. "No."

"You're on holiday then? Shopping?" Idonne was a country of artisans, healers, and scholars. The library, markets, and temple were renowned throughout the enchanted world.

"Yes," she lied once more.

"I wish I could escort you on a tour of the library," the young priest's tone was wistful. "But females aren't allowed inside the citadel."

She covered his hand—still holding the bowl full of food—with hers. "It's enough to stand at the gates and imagine the glory within."

A rose color suffused his cheeks. She bowed her head and released his hand. Before he could say anything else, she'd disappeared into the ruck on their way to the market.

A spike of pain split through the inside of Celeste's head; it felt as though someone had opened her skull and bludgeoned her brain with a hammer. Her screams drowned all meaning from the midwife's hushed words. The throbbing bolt redoubled its attack. A wave of black washed over her mind. When Celeste surfaced, the purpose of the stargazer's instructions were clear. Her fingers convulsed as she grabbed the midwife's hand. "You must promise to do what I ask!"

The kind woman pressed a damp cloth against the young mother's forehead. "If I can."

"Please! Don't defy my wishes with the notion that you know what is better for my child than his mother!"

The midwife stopped her ministrations to gaze into the young woman's eyes.

"I'm going to die in childbirth," Celeste said.

"There, there," the midwife said. "Let's have none of that talk."

Celeste raised herself up on her elbows and discharged a cry that was so stinging the midwife shrank back and covered her ears. On top of the hot spears impaling her head, it felt like someone carved into her abdomen with a razor-sharp dagger. "My son—" She dropped back into her sweat-soaked sheets, clutched her belly, and wailed again.

"Your son will be here before night falls."

It was late in the afternoon. The sun would set in a few hours. Celeste grabbed the midwife's bony wrist and squeezed it as hard as she could.

The woman's face contorted.

"You must do as I tell you. Please! Don't fail me in this!"

The midwife tilted her chin.

The slight gesture didn't settle Celeste's mind. She gritted her teeth. If the woman didn't do as she asked, all would be lost. "Tell me you will do what I ask!"

"Please, focus on your delivery, not what comes after."

"There will be no after for me!"

The midwife clucked as she massaged the knots in Celeste's belly.

The mother felt her life force ebbing. "Promise me," her hoarse voice rasped, "that when he is born, you'll take him to the Order of the Idonnai." With her last remnant of energy, Celeste stayed

12

the midwife's kneading hand and pointed to the infant-sized container sitting on the stone floor a few feet away. "I bought that basket for him. Every morning the priests give alms to the poor. Take my son and leave him there. They will not let him die."

"The pain has made you delirious."

"Promise me!"

"You would abandon your child?"

"His father"—Celeste closed her eyes as another contraction knifed her belly. She had no strength left to scream— "his father will recognize him in time and guarantee his future. There is nothing I can bequeath my son except life. Promise me." Had she even spoken the final words out loud?

The Delphinus choir sang as they always did at twilight. Their mysterious harmony filled the birth room with spiritual hope and yearning. Celeste's spirit soared. She envisioned her soul climbing the peak of Mount Azyllai. The pain that made her delivery so difficult melted away. The gods would bless her son.

Rays of eternal light parted the threatening wall of shadows. Celeste's final thoughts were of the fine reed basket, pale downy blanket, and luminous seashell rattle nestled therein. In her mind's eye, her newborn son gripped the kingly noisemaker and beamed. At peace, her thrashing abated.

13

The singing of the choir continued as the midwife called for the temple surgeon.

Koldis

Anton bowed his head in a show of obeisance.

Cashel, the head of the Order of the Idonnai, motioned him to sit.

The young priest settled in an unadorned chair. Three similar chairs, a large desk, and single overfull bookcase in matching blond wood gave the large room an empty feel. The impoverished appearance was a calculated display, for the priesthood was wealthy.

As if to confirm that point, the elder priest removed a dull leather pouch from the desk. He passed it from hand to hand. The unmistakable clink of coins filled the silence between the two men. "We've received word from Typhos," Cashel said. "A sailor claims to possess an artifact of great interest to us. If the offer proves genuine, I'd like you to purchase it for the library's collection."

Although he was curious as to what the object might be, Anton didn't ask. Reticence was a trait valued by the Order, and the young priest had long molded his character to gain approval from his superiors. He remained silent as he held out his hand.

Cashel made as if to give him the bag. His hand froze. "You must speak of this to no one."

"Of course not." The weight of the bag hit Anton's palm. Gold. He would be required to make an accounting of the coins upon his return. He counted them out now while the elder priest watched. He raised his eyebrows.

"You're authorized to negotiate the price of the sale. However, I prefer you pay all the gold in that bag than let the artifact be sold to another buyer."

Anton's subtle smile was genuine. To be trusted with such a mission assured his continued rise in the Order's hierarchy. "No one else will gain it."

"The broker will meet you at The Crossroads. You're familiar with the tavern?"

The Crossroads was a tavern in Maris, the busiest seaport in the enchanted world, and the capital of Typhos—one of two countries that bordered Idonne. On horseback, it was a two-day trip over mountain passes.

"Yes."

"I thought so. The broker will introduce himself as Ryko."

"When shall I depart?"

"Immediately. And stop by the aviary. Take one of the falcons with you as a safeguard."

When he reached Maris, Anton stabled his spent horse at one of the cheaper establishments on the outskirts of town. The overcast skies threatened a day of rain, but he felt less conspicuous on foot, less likely to be identified as a priest violating the Idonnic prohibitions against gaming, drinking, and coupling. After directing the falcon, Xeno, to stay close—but not too close—a man with a bird on his shoulder made for a memorable image and Anton had no desire to be remembered—the priest aimed for the city's center.

With his hood pulled close over his head, his thoughts turned to his mortal lover, Celeste. It had been months since their last tryst. Most priests never left the citadel in Idonne. Aesthetically, the city's white, marble architecture embodied the Order's faith in the purity of knowledge. Physically, the imposing structures shielded their inhabitants from the harsh Idonne sun, dry winds that blew regularly from the south, and the blazing sand that infiltrated almost every part of the country. The priests appreciated their precise and ordered world, perceiving its isolation as a benefit rather than a constraint.

For the past several years, Anton had curried favor with his superiors by volunteering for trips that others balked at. He'd discovered an unexpected advantage: The many temptations his excursions offered. The scattered afternoons and nights he'd spent with Celeste were the headiest. As he hiked toward the inn where she maintained a room, his other concerns faded. Anxious for her touch and the feel of her skin against his, he lost awareness of his surroundings, and the black-and-white-flecked falcon that hopped along the side of the road from one tall evergreen tree to the next.

The whistle of a pipe broke through Anton's consuming fantasies of Celeste. He walked along an isolated bend in the road. Someone or something scuffled behind him. The priest turned, but his reflexes were slow. A blow to the back of his head caused his knees to buckle.

He awoke at night, in a ditch, without shoes or cloak. The pouch of gold was gone. The base of his neck throbbed. He winced as his fingers palpitated the swollen knot between his shoulders. What a fool!

He swayed to his knees. By the two moons' placement, it was late, and the stretch of road was empty. It wasn't the place where he'd been attacked. His robbers must have dumped him here. He struggled to his feet and whistled for Xeno. The falcon didn't answer. Anton staggered through the quiet night, resolved to recover from this disaster. Returning to Idonne without the artifact wasn't an option.

He mounted the steps that led to Celeste's room and knocked upon her door. He rapped the wood with greater force. "It's Anton!" Someone inside the room groaned. "Celeste!" he shouted.

The door swung open. The priest stared into a muscled chest, thatched with dark hair. "There is no Celeste here!"

Anton ducked beneath the man's arm, forcing his way into the room.

"Hey, now! What are you doing?"

A stunned Anton circled the room. Every evidence of Celeste was gone: the wardrobe stuffed with her dresses and shoes, the vials of cosmetics and perfume lining the counter beneath the room's single mirror, the colorful scarves she draped across the window. Even the scent of her which had always perfumed the space had evaporated. It was as if she'd never existed. "Where is she?"

The man shook his head in negation. "This is my room now. Whoever lived here before, it's none of my business."

Anton turned in circles. "Impossible."

"Take it up with the landlord in the morning. Now get out of my room before I throw you out!"

Outside, it had begun to drizzle. Anton spent the rest of the night huddled beneath a cart on the side of the road. In the morning, the sound of its creaking wheels woke him. The cart pulled away, leaving him exposed. He swayed to his feet. Passersby stared. He obscured his face with his palm as he aimed for the inn.

The landlord's distasteful expression heightened his miserable state.

"Don't you recognize me?" Anton asked.

The man squinted. "Ah. You're one of Celeste's friends." His eyes settled on the priest's bare feet. "Rough night?"

"I was robbed."

"The thieves become bolder every day."

The information was of little use to Anton now. "Where is

Celeste?"

"How long has it been since your last visit?"

"Several months. The trip to Maris isn't a convenient one for me to make."

"Celeste's been gone awhile."

"Do you know where she went?"

"When they don't offer, I don't ask."

An image of her round face, vivacious green eyes, pouting lips, and mass of dark, curly hair laughed in Anton's mind. He pressed his fingers against his eyelids to quell the dull throb that promised a headache. Damn the temptation of her! If he'd not strayed from his mission to see her, he'd be on his way home now, artifact in hand. And yet he was anxious to know what had become of her. The thought of her sated in another man's arms sickened his gut like a meal of foul meat. "Was she alone when she left?"

"Now that you mention it, an older woman accompanied her. A healer from the temple in Idonne, perhaps. She wore one of those sea-colored robes."

Anton's chest constricted. There was no association between the occult practices of the priestesses who served the Temple of Delphinus and the scholarly pursuits of the male priests who served the Order of the Idonnai, but there were social relationships. If Celeste arrived in the marble citadel, confessing their liaison, it would be the end of his ambitions. Did she intend to destroy him? He pounded his fist against his forehead. The temple had a sanatorium. Perhaps her health suffered. "Was she ill?"

"No, I don't think it was that."

"Then what?"

The innkeeper rubbed his belly.

Anton raised his palm, in question.

"My guess? She was with child."

The young priest stumbled out to the street and glared at the rising sun. Traffic jostled him as he tried to absorb the news the innkeeper had given him. Celeste with child? Whose child? His? Dedicated solely to pursuits of the mind, the priests of Idonne didn't procreate. If the child was his, no one could ever know. Maybe it was better that she'd disappeared.

Anton's eyes darted among the crowd as he headed toward the docks. The streets of Maris were as full of foreigners as Typhons: warriors from Morganna, knights from Huros, sorcerers from Kyrakkos, a knot of dwarves from Misgradde or the Realm of Faerie—one could never be sure these days. He even spotted a toothless hag from the Black Magic Islands.

The young priest, who more resembled a down-on-his-luck deck hand at this point, spent the rest of the morning on the quay, observing. Lurking in the shadows, slipping between stacked crates, and blending in with the crews that loaded and unloaded ship cargo, he searched for the right candidate. By mid-afternoon, he settled on a wiry Typhon who displayed skill with a knife—he'd gutted a whole fish with the flick of a wrist—possessed a coarse nature—he'd issued vulgar insults to every female within shouting distance—and had physically menaced anyone who'd dared encroach upon his turf. He bared his teeth as Anton approached him.

The priest held up his hands. "I have a proposition for you."

The man growled.

"Allow me to buy you a mug of bitters," Anton offered. Several of the barkeeps at The Crossroads would extend him credit, he was sure.

The man took in Anton's bare head and feet. "Not thirsty."

"I won't waste your time."

"You already have."

Anton didn't deceive himself. He couldn't recover the stolen gold without help. The kind of help he suspected this stubborn Typhon could provide. "I have a proposal that could greatly benefit you."

"Not unless you're a genie who can grant me three wishes." The swarthy man snorted. "And you're not that."

"It's true, I'm no genie, but I can change your life."

The man wiped his forehead. Maris' sticky heat left everyone damp with sweat this time of day.

"What harm can come from sharing a cold mug with me at The Crossroads?" Anton held out his hand and introduced himself.

"You're either stubborn or dimwitted." The man crushed the bones in the priest's hand with a vise-like grip. "Bardo."

Anton maintained an impassive mask and forced himself to remain upright as a sharp pain radiated up his arm.

The Crossroads was the only establishment in Maris that served ice cold drinks. After the owner had discovered an ice foot off the northern coast of Typhos, he'd developed a method to transport large blocks of it overland. The ice was stored in bins insulated with thick layers of mud. As a result, The Crossroads had become the most popular drinking hole in Maris.

Anton appreciated the veil of anonymity as they waded through the knots of drinkers. He waited until they were seated to share his plan.

"A guard," Bardo mused.

"I visit Maris from time to time. Apparently, one cannot travel the streets without getting assaulted. Not even in daylight."

The man laughed. "You're an easy target."

"Perhaps. However, as a priest, I'm not trained in self-defense. We're prohibited from taking any action that might be interpreted as interfering with an organic unfolding of the Whole."

"What kind of bunk is that?"

"The Order of the Idonnai collects and protects vast resources of information. That knowledge puts us in a superior position."

"Superior to who?"

"To those who don't have access to our vaults. We observe, chronicle, and document, but never act. We take an oath to that effect. If we were to exploit the information others generously offer, well, they wouldn't be so eager to share their secrets with us."

Bardo swung his head in an unbelieving pendulum.

"That is where you come in." Anton had had most of the day to embellish his idea. "I'm interested in something more than a bodyguard. Perhaps a trained contingent, housed in Idonne, with members available to travel when necessary. The Order would provide equipment, uniforms, and barracks within the citadel.

You'd have everything you require to train recruits—"

"How much pay?"

Anton had no doubt he could sell his plan to Cashel if he rearranged the details of his assault. But the actual salary would have to be negotiated in Idonne. He could make one promise, though. "The captain of the guard will be paid in gold."

"If we cross the mountains, and I find out you're playing me, I'll bash your head in myself."

"I assure you that won't happen." Anton had already begun formulating the arguments to win Cashel over to his idea. The presence of a force of fighters in Idonne would fortify the citadel's security, safeguard their accumulation of wealth, and increase the Order's prestige throughout the enchanted world. The brotherhood's pretense of humility was just that. Celebrated as a body of enlightenment, they embraced every opportunity to expand their reputation. "But there is a matter of great urgency I must attend to before we leave for Idonne."

"What's that?" Bardo grunted.

Completing the task Cashel had assigned was Anton's top priority. Dealing with whether or not Celeste intended to destroy him would have to wait until he was back in Idonne. As much pleasure as he'd experienced in her bed, he would count himself lucky if he never saw her again. "I need to recover the gold that was stolen from me yesterday."

Bardo guffawed. "Whoever rolled you probably caught a ship at dawn. You'll never see those coins again."

Patrons at the nearest table glanced in their direction. Anton flinched. "Maybe. Maybe not. But I can't leave Maris until I'm sure."

"Even if your thief is still in Typhos, how do you expect to find him? Did you even see who hit you?"

"No, but there was a witness."

Bardo's gaze searched beyond Anton's shoulder. "And who might that be?"

"Let's go outside."

"Let's go inside and have a drink. Let's go outside and find my gold. Is this some kind of game?" Bardo asked.

"No game. If you help me recover my gold, I'll be indebted to you."

The wiry man drained his class and slapped the table. "I like the sound of that."

Anton crossed the road and a sward of thick grass to stand beneath a grove of towering evergreen trees. He whistled for Xeno. Again the falcon didn't answer his call.

"If I didn't know that was you singing, I'd think it was a bird," Bardo marveled.

"Priests are trained in birdsong. A falcon traveled with me yesterday. It's likely the bird saw the robber and followed him."

"Huh," Bardo grunted.

"Let's head back to the city center. I'll call Xeno along the way."

The falcon didn't show itself until they'd reached the approximate spot where Anton had returned to consciousness the night before.

When the bird lighted on the priest's shoulder, Bardo said, "Maybe you're not a liar."

Xeno and Anton whistled back and forth. "He can lead us to the thieves' lair," Anton told Bardo.

"Thieves? As in more than one?"

Anton ignored the question as the falcon lifted in the air to fly above their heads. The priest hurried after the bird, trusting that Bardo would be curious enough to follow. He was. Every so often, the falcon waited upon a low branch for the pair to catch up.

Xeno led them north. The population dwindled. They reached a wooded area where Anton and Bardo thrashed through increasingly dense undergrowth, slapping at flying insects that stung every patch of their exposed skin. The barely visible bites itched until they were scratched raw. Sharp rocks buried beneath the mush of dead leaves bruised Anton's heels and scraped his bare soles. He crouched and contorted his body under rough tree limbs and around giant trunks. The dank air seemed more suffocating in the darkening shade. Sweat trickled from Anton's brow and stained his shirt and breeches. His own ripe smell made him long for his pristine existence in the citadel.

Xeno returned to Anton's shoulder. The priest translated the bird's report to Bardo. "Two sand gypsies have taken a dwarf hostage. They're forcing him to craft magical trinkets with whatever gold they steal. They store their plunder in a cave, near the shore."

"Sand gypsies are dangerous folk. They may be slight in build, but they're tricky with their shell pipes and colored sand, dyed with magic. Blown directly in the eyes, it's temporarily blinding. They can do just about whatever they want with you then."

Anton rubbed the back of his neck. "If we're quick, we won't have to face them. They've left for the day's looting. Xeno will lead us to the cave where the dwarf is chained, working at his forge. You'll need to search inside for the gold while I stand guard. I need every one of the hundred pieces they stole back. But take no more than that."

Bardo's eyes widened. "Why leave the rest?"

"If you leave some of their haul, maybe they won't notice we were there until we've left Maris." He hoped. "There's no need to be greedy."

"What if that's all the gold there is?"

"Then take it!"

"And if they come looking for us?"

The possibility of being blinded and tortured made Anton's stomach queasy. "You're handy with that knife hanging from your belt."

Bardo picked up on Anton's discomfort and grinned. "Using it won't interfere with the 'organic unfolding of the Whole'?"

"As long as I don't cut their throats, we'll be good."

Bardo chortled. "I'm beginning to understand why you brought me along."

The last leg of their trek was painstaking. They took deliberate steps across uneven ground and slid down ravines. Many of the inclines were so steep they had to grab roots to climb up the other side. The terrain, so taxing for Anton and Bardo, would present little challenge to the sand gypsies, known to be dexterous with both hands and feet. Nomads who sailed from beach to beach, they scuttled like crabs on land. The potent magic they brewed with elements from the Great White Sea aided their thievery and made their capture impossible. When a tribe settled on the beach of any country in the enchanted world, they simply had to be endured by the local populace until they sailed away in their large, flat-bottomed arks.

Anton muttered thanks to the gods of Azyllai at the sound and smell of the sea. Despite their slow progress and the sun falling in the sky, the gypsies still hadn't returned to their cave.

Smoke curled from the black hole in a grass-covered hill. Bardo was going to have to bend in half to enter. Anton's heart thumped as he watched the tall man crawl through the small opening. Once he disappeared from view, the priest crouched next to the entrance. The sound of banging metal drifted from the interior. It stopped. Muffled voices followed. Anton poked his head inside the cave, straining to hear the conversation, but it was useless. His eyes adjusted to the dark. Mounds of cloth, piles of bones, and a couple of animal carcasses formed haphazard masses on a dusty floor blotched with mud puddles. If the dwarf was crafting valuables, they were stored deeper in the cave. There was nothing enticing in the fetid room his eyes searched. Disgusted, the priest backed away.

He gulped deep breaths of fresh air as he stared into the forest. The faint melody of a pipe and laughter reached his ears. Anton rushed back to the cave opening. "Bardo! Bardo!"

A high-pitched banging rose from the cave's belly. Overhead, Xeno circled and squawked. The priest straightened. Bardo needed time. Desperate to assure his partner's success, Anton oriented himself to the approaching sounds and strode at an angle guaranteed to cross their path. Although he marched with purpose, chill perspiration made his body clammy. He thought he might faint.

Anton froze. A bent-over creature blocked his path. A royal-blue bandana held back long, oily hair. An emerald cloak covered the gypsy's malformed shape. The creature muttered something. An enchantment? The gypsy swayed from side to side as his hand disappeared in the swirl of cloth that enveloped him. A glassy sheen in the gypsy's eyes riveted Anton's attention. The priest tried to speak, but his words spilled out in a senseless jumble. The gypsy's hand darted like a snake. A twinkling of sand dusted the priest's temple and cheek. Tiny crystalline grains entered his nostrils and grated against the surface of his eyes. He sneezed and blinked. When he opened his eyes, the world was black around him.

The pipe's melody stopped.

"Heh. What have we here, Endahl?" A high-pitched voice asked.

"Hmm. A scout is what I'm thinking, Urtahl." The voice was much deeper.

Xeno screeched from atop a tree.

"Do you think that's his falcon?"

"Could be."

"Should we shoot it before the nuisance reveals our location to someone else?"

"Would make a tasty bite of dinner."

Xeno fell silent.

"What are you doing in these woods?" Urtahl's squeaky voice circled the priest.

"Only taking a walk." At last he'd found his voice, although it rattled like a wire in the wind.

A hard rod slammed the back of Anton's calf. Probably the same staff that had struck him yesterday. The priest crashed forward. He landed, palms and knees in the mud, humiliated. Without sight, he was helpless to defend himself. "Am I trespassing on your land? I didn't realize."

A heel shoved Anton's buttocks. The priest sprawled forward, his face landing in a foul paste of dirt and stagnant water. Anton sputtered the filth from his tongue as he struggled to rise. Claw-like fingers dug into his scalp and jerked his head up. Up. Up.

"He looks familiar," Urtahl said.

The steamy hotness of breath struck Anton's cheek. His blood thundered in his ears.

"All these land dwellers look the same to me," Endahl grumbled.

"I mean no harm," Anton pleaded. "I'm a priest!"

"Sure you are." Endahl's sharp fingers probed Anton's pockets before poking his neck and wrists, presumably hoping to find a gold or silver chain. "Nothing." He spat on the ground. "Maybe he's what he says. Vows of poverty and all."

Urtahl pulled Anton's head even higher, straining his neck. "What's a priest doing out here in the middle of nowhere?"

"Contemplation." Without sight, Anton was quickly becoming attuned to sound. He heard movement in the brush, something tinkling and racing through the undergrowth. Dogs with jangling collars? Frightened horses with bells upon their harnesses? "Did you hear that?"

Urtahl dropped his head and jumped to his feet to search the thicket. Endahl joined him. Anton strained to understand what they mumbled to one another as he staggered to his feet.

They turned and advanced upon him again. Endahl shoved his chest. "You need to do your contemplation in some other woods," he sneered.

Anton agreed with a vigorous nod.

Urtahl matched the priest's every backward step with a forward lunge. "Get out of here!" he commanded shrilly. "If we see you lurking in these parts again"—cold metal pressed against Anton's throat—"we'll carve you up and throw you in a soup pot. Got it?"

"Yes," Anton whispered.

"What's that?" Erdahl boomed in Anton's ear. "We can't hear you!"

"Yes!" he yelled.

The sand gypsies exploded with derisive laughter. "Look how white his face is!" Urtahl jeered. He pushed the priest a final time.

If he escaped with his life, Anton would never leave the safety of the citadel again! Let some other fool risk his life as a glorified errand boy. He stumbled once more before he found his feet. Running blindly, tripping, lurching; his heart pounded as he freed himself from the clutches of assailants that transformed into

35

leafless branches. He tumbled headfirst into ravines and wriggled on his belly to ascend the other side. He continued his spasmodic escape long after the gypsies' laughter faded. When his throat burned from ragged breathing, and he couldn't crawl any further on his sliced hands and bruised knees, he wilted to the ground.

The gold. His future. Celeste. All was lost. He curled into a ball.

Xeno whistled.

Anton opened his eyes.

Bardo kneeled over him. "What happened to you?"

The priest pushed himself to sitting. He rubbed his eyes. The world, black when he'd passed out, was filled with blurred shadows. "I can see!"

The Typhon rocked back on his heels, metal clanking. "The gypsies got you, did they?"

"They were returning to the cave. I had to create a distraction. How did you find me?"

"The bird."

"You followed it?"

"Not me." Bardo pointed to a squat figure beside him.

Anton strained to distinguish an uneven silhouette, but a grey mask concealed the details of form and face. He glanced around, fearful that the sand gypsies' magic had left him in a murky world of black-and-white. But the forest's dulled browns, greens, reds, and yellows showed themselves in the day's fading light. Anton refocused on Bardo and his companion—a dwarf. With great relief he realized their faces and limbs—and everything they wore—were blackened with soot and ash. The only bright points to their shapes were the whites of their eyes, and the swords and knives strapped around their chests and across their backs.

"You have the gold?" Anton's voice quavered.

"All of it."

"I'm surprised you came back for me."

The man shrugged. "When I was boy, I dreamed of living a life with honor, just never had the chance. Rough beginnings and all —"

"He saved me," the dwarf interrupted. "They kidnapped me. Kept me in chains. Bardo picked the lock. I'm free." The short creature's weapons clanged as he hopped in an energetic circle.

Bardo dropped something in Anton's lap. It was the pouch. The priest hefted it in his hand. He could tell by its weight that Bardo hadn't stolen a coin. "I'll do everything in my power to assure you become the first captain of the Idonnai Guard." He'd never been more sincere about anything in his life.

Bardo grinned. "I like the sound of that."

"We need to get to the baths before they close," the dwarf said. "This soot and grime has served its purpose, the gypsies haven't been able to track us. But the odor is turning carious. No offense, Mr. Priest, but you don't smell so fine either. No respectable establishment will serve us in this condition, and all I can think of us is tucking into a nice roast. I've existed on nothing but cold gruel and tinny-tasting water for more than a moon cycle."

Anton checked his body and found only superficial cuts and bruises. "Lead the way," he said to the dwarf. Better to be washed and fed before he attended to his business.

The dwarf had pocketed enough treasure from the cave to generously reward Bardo; book himself passage to Misgradde; and finance baths, fresh clothes, and a celebratory meal for the trio. At the end of their feast, he announced his wish to leave Typhos as soon as possible. "I can't risk being recaptured by those thugs."

Bardo volunteered to escort him to the docks. Stuffed, and reeking of incense from the bath's public steam room, the three unlikely companions strode the city street abreast. When they reached The Crossroads, Anton bid them farewell. Bardo would meet the priest at the stables on the edge of Maris in the morning.

Anton watched Xeno fly across a field to perch in a tall evergreen tree. With a newfound appreciation for his ability to see, he found himself paying attention to details he'd never bothered to notice before. After gazing at the stars overhead, he fell in line with the stream of customers entering the ramshackle tavern.

Settled at a table in the corner, Anton's fingers gripped an icy mug of bitters. Appreciating the slick, wet film on the glass, he raised it to his lips. As a member of the Order of the Idonnai, he wasn't supposed to imbibe. Perhaps the perils of the day had been some sort of supernatural reckoning for his violations. Well, he'd had enough adventure for one lifetime. When he returned to Idonne, he would stay there.

"Did Cashel send you?"

The rough voice returned Anton to the matter at hand. "I am his agent."

The man, short and dark, eased into the seat across from the priest. He introduced himself as Ryko. When the barmaid came by, the sea-weathered man ordered two more glasses of bitters. Anton didn't protest. His mug was empty.

After the young girl delivered two more icy mugs, Ryko said,

"I've sailed all over the enchanted world and cultivated some rewarding contacts. What I'm about to show you is singular. For a prize like this to surface is rare." He placed a long, narrow package on the table.

Anton's heart pumped.

Ryko observed their surroundings. No one appeared to be paying their shadowy corner any especial attention. He tugged at the parcel's string and unfolded a bit of the canvas covering. A faint blue light shimmered.

Anton pulled the object closer. He doubted the dwarf Bardo had saved this afternoon would have been so quick to sail from Typhos had he known the sword Koldis was in Maris.

In the enchanted world it was often hard to distinguish fact from fiction. Anton had always believed the tale of the two dwarves Haff and Gweff to be a scrap of myth or legend. But now, the great sword lay on the table before him.

In an effort to negotiate the best price, Anton quizzed Ryko relentlessly. He could find no inconsistencies in the man's story.

The grizzled sailor pointed to the bundle between them. "I recognized the superb craftsmanship right off, but I've held on to it for a long time. Now, I'm ready to settle down. I figure a fair price for the sword will secure my future."

Anton haggled, but Ryko knew the value of the blade.

The priest slouched. He would deliver Koldis to the Order, but not at a bargain price. He dropped the pouch of gold Bardo had recovered that afternoon into the sailor's open palm.

The next morning, Anton skulked through the alleys, searching for someone young and hungry. He came upon a gang of urchins hunched over a street game. They were thin and dirty. He watched them play, noting their mannerisms and expressions. One struck him as particularly cruel. When their game ended, he shadowed the boy.

After several turns, the lad whipped around. "What do you want?"

"Are you handy with that slingshot?" Anton asked.

"Yeah. So?"

Anton crouched to whisper in the boy's ear. He couldn't risk Xeno overhearing his proposition. "You see the bird with the speckled feathers on that branch over there?"

The boy lifted his head, searching. He nodded.

Anton pushed a piece of copper into his hand. "I need you to kill it."

The boy grinned.

The priest added a piece of silver to the boy's open palm. It tinkled against the smaller coin. "Tell no one about it."

"Can I eat the meat?" the boy asked.

"Do with the carcass what you will."

The falcon was a loose end Anton could ill afford when he fabricated the story of his assault for Cashel. And if Celeste meant to confess their assignations to the Order, he must be able to deny everything.

The Idonnqi Gyqrd

The blood-red stone drew Ryder's gaze. A rush of whispers flooded his mind, an eerie plea for aid? The seven-year-old boy's heart pounded in his chest. Did Anton hear the call? Ryder canted his head, withdrawing his gaze from the hilt of the magnificent sword. The troubling echoes silenced.

The priest stood beside him, erect in his sand-colored robes, with hands clasped in front of his body. "The blade is named Koldis," Anton said. "It's said to possess magical properties."

"Does it?"

"Perhaps." The sword rested on a cushion fashioned from crimson velvet within a glass casing. Other than the pedestal, the room was empty.

Ryder returned his gaze to the sword. This time he ignored the ruby and his mind remained silent as he studied the length of the blade. The faintest blue light shimmered from the metal. He took a step closer to the glass case enshrining the artifact. "Why is it here, where no one can use it to fight?"

"How many times must I tell you? Idonnic priests do not fight!"

The boy yearned for adventure. He intended to be as different from the man standing next to him as possible. He risked another peek at the blade's hilt. A whirlwind of unintelligible whispers again stirred his mind. Mesmerized by the ruby, he longed to take the sword and run, to carry the blade far beyond the library's white marble walls. "Can I have it?" he whispered.

"And what would you do with it, if it were yours?" Anton asked.

"I would conquer all my enemies."

"Idonnic priests do not have enemies."

Ryder shrugged. "Everyone has enemies."

The priest crouched beside the young boy. "What have I told you about your temper?"

"That I must learn to control it," the boy mumbled.

"And why must you control it?"

"Because Idonnic priests do not fight," Ryder mimicked the mantra in a monotone.

"That is correct. We observe, we record, we document. And we

44

never interfere."

Ryder pulled his gaze from the red gemstone. "I'm not going to be a priest."

Anton's eyebrows raised in warning.

"I'm never going to be a priest!"

Anton struck Ryder with the side of his closed fist.

The boy wobbled. The flow of blood surged in his veins. He shook his head to clear the ringing from his ears. Anton only hit him when they were alone. Ryder lowered his head, shifted his weight, and slammed his heel into Anton's shin.

The priest released a satisfying bellow.

The boy covered his mouth to hide his delighted smile.

Anton grabbed his young charge by the shirt and dragged him into the hall. Ryder tripped and slid on the polished marble floors. The priest didn't pause until they reached one of the courtyards where the Idonnai Guard trained. At the sight of the tall black whipping post, Ryder twisted, but his mentor's grip was a vise.

Anton shouted for Bardo.

The muscled captain of the Idonnai Guard appeared.

The priest spoke through clenched teeth, "Perhaps some lashes will remind this one of the proper deportment."

The captain returned with a black whip and length of rope.

Ryder's lower lip trembled. He wouldn't shame himself by crying. He walked to the whipping post and hugged it. Bardo tethered his wrists and ankles. The young boy clamped his mouth shut.

"Make him scream!" Anton exhorted.

Bardo hesitated.

"Harder!"

The whip's sting sharpened. Ryder wished for Garrick, the man he thought of as a father. His name slipped from Ryder's mouth.

"What did you say?" Anton asked.

Garrick, who supplied the Order with loaves of bread every morning before dawn, had been the one to find the infant abandoned outside the citadel gates seven years ago. The baker and his wife were Ryder's only respite from Anton's smothering attention.

The boy mouthed the name once more, although no sound came out.

By the time Anton was satisfied with the punishment, Ryder hung limply in his restraints.

Eleven years later, Ryder rose before the sun. The quiet dormitory beyond his closet-sized room bolstered his resolve.

The need to move, to test his strength, to develop some sort of physical prowess grew in him like an out-of-control appetite. He couldn't sit through one more lecture in respectful silence, stare for hours at one more dusty parchment, or feign interest in another theory about "something" without challenging his muscles, or working up a good sweat. His mind was exhausted while his body craved movement. His hands fumbled as he slipped on the pair of dark trousers and work shirt he'd stolen from the laundry room.

That Anton wouldn't be pleased with his plan made it that much more appealing.

Ryder pulled aside the sand-colored curtain that served as a door for the cramped, private sleeping space afforded every student of the Order. His peers still slept. He counted none of them as friends—to be scholars, to be trained to serve as agents of the Idonnic Library fulfilled their ambitions. They believed themselves honored—not imprisoned by some unkind fate. None could understand Ryder's need for physical exertion. He never tried to explain it anymore.

Without the traditional sandals worn as part of every student's uniform, Ryder's footsteps were soundless. At the end of the hall, he paused to quell his thumping heart. When he was satisfied no one followed him, he pressed the lever to release the exterior door. Outside, he held its weight until the door closed. Then he tore across a parched field toward a long, low building—the Idonnai Guard barracks.

Despite the whippings Ryder had endured through the years, he'd taken to prowling around the outskirts of the guard's combat amphitheaters, gymnasiums, and training courtyards. Familiar with their daily schedule, he intended to create his own rudimentary training program. One he'd pursue like a ghost in the shadows.

He crouched as he advanced along the building to an inconspicuous door he knew was not locked. He eased it open and slipped inside.

A crowd of new recruits milled about. No one questioned his arrival because Ryder looked like he belonged in the class. The Idonnai were tall, thin, blue-eyed, and fair-haired. Ryder's shorter stature, dark hair, unusual green eyes, and utilitarian garments blended in with the rest of the foreigners attending their first day of training.

He strode casually to the back of the hall.

When the training officer entered and began barking commands, Ryder fell in line. He executed the physical drills with determination as the officer threaded his way through the ranks. The movements were basic and easy to follow. Ryder threw himself into the routine, relishing every squat, bend, and twist. When the citadel bell rang for the morning meal, Ryder froze. His paralyzed body drew the officer's attention. The rest of the recruits continued to move. Awkwardly, Ryder resumed the drill, his heart pounding. He'd been careless to react to the first chime for breakfast. The guard ate after the priests and students.

The officer approached the last row until he stood squarely in front of Ryder. "What are you doing here?"

"Training," Ryder said.

"I handpicked everyone in this class. I didn't pick you."

Ryder continued to drop to the floor, thrust his legs behind him, and bound back up to a standing position.

The officer ended the class.

Ryder offered a curt nod.

The officer blocked his exit. "How did you get in here?"

"I'm a priest, sir. A student," he quickly corrected. "I came from the dormitory."

The officer crossed his arms as he studied Ryder more closely. "Priests train their minds, not their bodies."

"I wish to train my body."

"Where did you get that uniform?"

"I took it from the laundry."

"A cheat and a thief," the officer barked.

"I don't wish to be a cheat or a thief. I wish to join the guard."

The heel of the officer's palm slammed into Ryder's rib cage. The young man lost his footing and collapsed to one knee. "How will you defend others when you can't defend yourself?" Before Ryder could regain his footing, the man slammed the side of Ryder's jaw with the heel of his other palm.

Ryder flew sideways into the dirt. "I want to learn to defend myself."

The man crouched and glared into his eyes. "You wouldn't have survived the tryouts. Get out of here."

The assessment scalded. Ryder pushed himself up.

"I don't ever want to see you in that uniform again. Return it to the laundry." The officer stalked off.

Ryder limped through the hall to exit through the same side door he'd entered earlier. Two recruits blocked his way. One was an impassive mountain, arms crossed over his chest; the other was smaller than his friend, but taller and more muscled than Ryder. He curled his lip and glared. "What made you think you could just sneak in here?"

"I made a mistake. Excuse me."

"Do you have any idea how many of our friends got rejected for this training?" the shorter recruit asked.

The mountain spit on Ryder's bare foot. "You insult us by wearing our training uniform."

Ryder made no effort to wipe off the saliva. His jaw throbbed, and the pain in the left side of his body made him want to curl in a ball on the floor. "I didn't mean to insult you, or your friends."

The mountain loomed closer. "You need to learn your place."

"The officer made it clear that I'm not welcome here." The pair squinted at Ryder, as if assessing how much more damage they could inflict on his already aching body. He held up his hands. "Please, let me pass. You must be hungry. Isn't it time for breakfast?"

The shorter recruit punched the mountain in the shoulder. "Are you hungry, Thessar?"

The mountain didn't budge, nor did he break eye contact with Ryder. "I am."

"Wouldn't it be nice to have someone serve us?" The shorter recruit snickered.

"Yes, it would."

Ryder's stomach sank as any hope of making friends among the guard vanished. The pair jabbed and poked him toward the door. Having reached his tolerance for physical pain, Ryder didn't resist.

In the dining hall he tried to make light of the humiliation. But when a sharp pain traveled from his armpit to his groin, the heavy tray weighted down with the demands of Thessar's enormous appetite slid from his hands. As Ryder's body folded in defense against the spasm, the tray and all the food on it smashed to the floor.

Hoots and jeers rang through the hall.

"You're useless!" Thessar cuffed Ryder's head. "Get out of here!"

Ryder hobbled to the now-empty dormitory where he exchanged his milk-stained shirt and porridge-streaked trousers for the standard issue robe worn by the Order's students. He stuffed the soiled uniform beneath his cot.

Ryder stood as tall as he could with his head raised. The brace he'd created from a ripped-up sheet helped to minimize the bruising shockwaves that rippled through his torso in a nauseating rhythm. His jaw smarted where the officer had struck him, but the room was not well-lit. Perhaps the swelling and discoloration wasn't visible from where Anton sat with his back rigid behind a gilded desk.

"Please, tell me it wasn't you who tried to train with the guard this morning."

"I cannot."

Anton's eyes, as pale blue as the sand phlox that sprouted in tenacious patches amid Idonne's sandy terrain, glared. "Please, sit."

Ryder didn't object; he needed to get off his feet. He advanced to one of two gold leaf chairs that faced Anton's desk. Easing his body down, Ryder carefully adjusted his spine against the chair's ornately scrolled back.

Where Cashel had favored austere surroundings as head of the Order, Anton believed in displaying the priesthood's wealth.

"Why didn't you ask me if you could train with them?" Anton asked.

"Would you have said yes?"

"No."

"That is why I didn't ask."

Anton chose the golden apple. Whenever anger threatened his priestly façade, he gripped one of the decorative objects arranged meticulously across his desk.

Ryder squelched his impulse to grab the porcelain statue of a miniature ship and toss it at Anton's head.

Curled around the apple, Anton's fingers were pale, his knuckles white. "Your eighteenth birthday is next week."

Ryder flinched. His birthday was celebrated on the day he'd been found at the priesthood gate. He preferred not to be reminded of his inauspicious beginnings. As far as he was concerned, fate had delivered him to the wrong doorstep. "I don't belong here. I'm no priest. I'm not a scholar—"

"Your teachers disagree. They praise your attention to detail and ability to synthesize disparate facts."

"Every other student of the Order is Idonne-born. Every other student wants to be here. I don't!" Ryder ignored the stabbing cramp as he leaned forward in his seat. "And you never tire of telling me that my temperament is not suited for the vocation of priest."

Anton set the golden apple down on the desk with a loud crack. "What will you do if you refuse to take your vow?"

"Join the guard!"

"They won't have you."

"Only because I have no experience in fighting."

"You would need my approval."

Ryder jerked back in his chair and winced.

Anton straightened the front of his robes and folded his hands before him on the desk. "You romanticize danger and risking your life. But the world beyond these walls is not what you think it is. You're safe here in the citadel—"

"A safety that is suffocating me. Must my body weaken and my spirit wither while I am still young?"

A shadow darkened Anton's pale blue eyes. "Fate brought you to the Order. You're a gifted scholar. And soon you'll be a gifted priest."

"I will soon be a man. One with ties to no family. I would choose my own future."

Anton pushed his chair back with a loud scrape. He stood up and leaned across his desk. "The Order of Idonnai has invested in you. We've fed you, sheltered you, and trained you. You owe us your allegiance." He paced.

"Your demand I pay with my life's blood for not drowning me like an unwanted kitten is unfair! I'm nothing more than a slave here."

Ryder didn't see Anton's hand, but he felt the crest of the ring cut his lip as his head jolted to the side. He relished the sting as he licked blood from his lip. The priest's strike lacked the power of the officer's.

Anton stepped back. "You will take your vow!"

Any gratitude or indebtedness Ryder had ever felt toward Anton or the priesthood leached from him. He controlled his impulse to pummel the priest, but his entire body shook with the effort. He would not take the Oath of Non-Interference, because he would never commit his mind, or his body, or his heart to a life of inaction. The knowing overflowed Ryder's heart like a gorged river swelling across the dry flats in Idonne's rainy season.

There was a knock at the door.

"Enter," Anton commanded.

The Captain of the Idonnai Guard made himself comfortable in the seat next to Ryder.

"Have you considered my request?" Anton asked.

"I've discussed it with the officers," Bardo said. "They're willing to work with you on the matter."

Anton resettled in his chair. "Ryder, joining the Order of the Idonnai is a great honor. One you've earned by overcoming significant obstacles. You'll be the first priest who isn't Idonne-born. I'll not allow you to squander your accomplishment for a foolish dream."

"But—"

Anton held up his hand. "However, I can see that you're determined to put yourself in harm's way. I've decided to indulge your self-destructive urges, and have asked Bardo to allow you to train with the guard–"

The blood pumped faster through Ryder's chest.

"On the condition that you take the Oath of Non-Interference with the rest of your class."

Ryder's mouth dried and he felt as though he'd swallowed a pail of sand.

Bardo picked at his rough, calloused hands. "I've promised Anton that there will be no training until you've said your vow. If we catch you lurking around the barracks before then, you'll be whipped."

"Well?" Anton asked. "Will you take the Oath?"

Was there any real choice before him? Had there ever been? Ryder choked out the word that would grant him what he'd always wanted, for a price he'd promised never to pay. "Yes."

❖ ❖ ❖

The annual commitment ceremony was the Order's event of the year. It was the only time females were allowed to enter the citadel.

In the week prior to the festivities, caravans from Typhos

trundled over the mountains. Weighted down with costumes, decorations, foodstuff, and performers, they creaked along Idonne's dusty roads.

As they filed through the golden gates, chaos descended. The Order's staid culture cartwheeled and landed on its head. Priestly conduct contorted like a flexible gymnast as members of the Order joined the intruding revelers in ribald and garish displays. Agog and laughing at the out-of-character antics, Ryder had always reveled in the madness. But this year, the festive preparations underscored the agreement he'd made with Anton.

He put in longer and longer hours in the library. After his assignments were complete, he searched for fantastical stories about heroes and their adventures.

Anton couldn't cage his mind.

The morning of the ceremony, Ryder decided the pretentious celebration was more suited to a coronation than a solemn vow that would effectively function as a death sentence. At least the novitiates were exempt from wearing the ridiculous paper capes and matching hats everyone else wore. It would be the first day they donned their official robes.

Along the way to the auditorium, street musicians blared carnival music. Food vendors hawked delicacies deemed too rich for the priests' palates the rest of the year. Inside the auditorium, a dizzying sea of blue, lavender, orange, pink, and yellow flowers carpeted the floor and every visible step and walkway. An endless length of gaudy tinsel draped the auditorium walls normally devoid of decoration.

Priests, artisans, craftsmen, market vendors, and the priestesses from the Temple of Delphinus packed into every seat. Acrobats twirled from great hoops that dangled from the high ceiling.

Anton sat in the gallery with other high-ranking priests and Bardo. As always, the Idonnai Guard—swelled to a rank of more than five-hundred members over the years—was the most rowdy group in the amphitheater. They'd been drinking flame-flower sap —prohibited within the citadel at all other times—since dawn.

Ryder stood in line with eight lean scholars. The shortest figure in the row, and the only one with dark hair and a square jaw, his lips were cracked and the collar of his sand-colored robe chafed.

A cleric blew the ivory horn. The muffled roar of more than a thousand voices silenced instantaneously. Anton rose and welcomed the audience. His was the only golden robe in the auditorium. Cashel had never sought such distinction, but it was no secret that Anton's ambitions far exceeded his predecessor's. Ryder was only surprised that his mentor didn't sport a matching crown.

"The Oath of Non-Interference requires an Idonnic Priest refrain from action," Anton's voice rang out beneath the amphitheater's dome. "The organic unfolding of the Whole is paramount. We are privy to esoteric, historic, and sacred information. This access must never be exploited. As members of the Order of the Idonnai, we chronicle and observe, discuss and theorize. Our extensive knowledge must never be profaned. A priest's life is one of ideals and self-discipline. Thus we are charged with a single vow that guides our every decision."

Anton called the name of the first candidate, who marched across the dais. He stopped below the galley, his head raised, meeting Anton's gaze. The head of the Order raised his right hand with his four fingers straight and his thumb flat across his palm. The candidate mirrored the posture. "Repeat after me," Anton said. "I will uphold the ideals of the priesthood."

The young man repeated the declaration proudly.

"I will dedicate my being to scholarly pursuits and a life of the mind."

Ryder's impulse was to flee, to rip off the sand-colored robe and escape the citadel forever. But where would he go?

"I will not trespass against the organic unfolding of the

Whole."

As each candidate was called forth, Ryder's thoughts rampaged against a barren future. His soul clamored for adventure. Heroism. Action—

Anton called Ryder's name. His feet traced the same path as those that had gone before him. No one seemed offended by his rote recitation.

"I will not violate the trust I bear as a sacred keeper of knowledge."

The damage was done. He'd betrayed himself. His existence was a lie.

He made a feeble effort to silence his self-recrimination. He paid this price to train with the guard.

✧ ✧ ✧

Anton led Ryder through an intricate labyrinth of halls and stairwells. When they reached a dark walnut door, the priest withdrew a strand of smoky glass beads from his robe. An over-sized brass key hung from the waist-length necklace. He used it to unlock the door.

The long, narrow room resembled almost every other room in the Idonnic Library: the white marble walls and visible floor gleamed; intricately designed rugs ran between rows of towering bookcases; bright light poured in from a tall window at the opposite end of the steepled ceiling.

Anton locked the door behind them. He gestured for Ryder to join him at a bench before a table pushed against the wall.

Ryder hesitated. All morning he'd waited for Anton's official notification to begin training with the guard. Bringing him to this isolated attic did nothing to assure Ryder that the elder priest intended to honor his word.

"This room contains a private collection," Anton said. "One that is of utmost importance to me."

The announcement pricked Ryder's curiosity, but he remained mute and suspicious as he settled onto the bench.

Anton continued, "There is a potency gathering in the Void."

The young priest shifted toward his mentor.

The elder priest seized upon his protege's reluctant interest. "Comprehension of this entity is imperative."

"Why? What is the purpose of comprehension and analysis if we can never interfere?"

"We're not prohibited from communicating our knowledge—"

Or selling it, Ryder had recently learned.

"We also develop theories. However, in order to do so with intelligence, one's thought processes must be grounded in fact.

The history that has led to this entity's unprecedented evolution will provide the necessary foundation: The beginning is in the seed. Initially, as you study these scattered events, they might seem unrelated. I doubt they will appear so by the end. Do you have any questions?"

Ryder could bite his tongue no longer. "When will my training with the guard begin?"

Anton tapped his little finger and thumb against the tabletop. "You must understand that the members of the guard have been screened for certain traits—raw physical strength and ruthlessness among them. Although the training emphasizes the development of character, integrity, and discipline, most recruits arrive at the citadel with unsavory qualities. The guard offers them a chance to change their fortunes. But have no illusions, they're a rough group. If you choose to go forward with this training, neither Bardo nor I can guarantee your safety."

The temperature of Ryder's blood rose a degree with every word. "We have an agreement."

"Yes, we do. But I won't hold you to it, if you'd like to bow out now."

"I have no desire to bow out."

"As long as you understand the risks."

Ryder could have seized Anton by the stiff collar of his robe and shaken him until his teeth rattled. "I understand," he gritted out the words.

The elder priest broke eye contact. "You're granted permission to attend the endurance drills at sunrise, and the ring-training sessions at sunset. If your research suffers, my permission will be withdrawn."

At last! The chance to train with the most elite group of soldiers in the enchanted world. Memories of Thessar's humiliation receded. Ryder would make a fresh start. A rare grin broke open his mouth. "Thank you."

"Shall we return to a discussion of your primary responsibilities?"

"Yes."

Anton removed the beaded strand from his neck. "You'll begin tomorrow with a study of the birth of the Whole. Each day your required reading will be arranged on this table when you arrive. Leave your notes on the parchment that will also be provided." Anton held out the key.

Ryder's eyes widened as he opened his palm.

"As my duties are extensive, it will be a rare occasion when I'll be able to join you as I've done today." He dropped the key in

Ryder's hand. "Keep it concealed as I have done."

It wouldn't be sailing the Great White Sea, but at least the assignment held the promise of mental adventure. And tonight, he would beginning his training. "Yes, sir."

A few minutes after Ryder entered the training courtyard, Bardo approached him. "I usually don't attend these sessions, but I wanted to give you a pointer." The man's beard was speckled with grey, and his build was deceptively slight. Although more compact and older than his officers, he was solid muscle. Once Ryder had come upon him in an isolated gymnasium and watched in awe as he'd performed a daring one-handed acrobatic drill that Ryder had never seen any other member of the guard perform.

The recruits parted as Bardo led Ryder to the edge of the ring. There, the guard's captain folded his arms and watched the two fighters. They both had dark hair, but one's was shorn close to his skull, while the other's was a rat's nest of curls. Ryder judged they were from Typhos and Morganna, respectively. Typhons were leaner, with rounder faces. Morgannai were thicker and meaner.

After dancing around the ring a couple of times, the Typhon fisted a swift one-two punch. The Morgannai dodged both easily, bent over, aimed his head square to his opponent's abdomen, and rammed forward. The Typhon twisted so the blow only glanced his ribcage. The pair continued to bob around the ring.

"They're both skilled fighters," Bardo said. "But the Morgannai are gifted with something like a second-sight in physical combat. They can see their attacker make a fist a split second before he clenches his hand. It gives them a great advantage. But that other boy is doing me and my fellow countrymen proud."

"What about when weapons are used? Does that alter a Morgannai's gift?"

"Good question." Bardo clapped Ryder on the shoulder. "Indeed it does. The Morgannai's second-sight is blind to any hand holding metal. The metal seems to conduct an energy current that interrupts their pre-vision."

"Then why do you pair the other recruits with the Morgannai in these training sessions? It hardly seems fair when they have such an advantage?"

The Typhon was pinned on his back as the Morgannai pummeled his face. A gush of blood spewed from the Typhon's nose before the ring-minder called the contest for the Morgannai.

"Fair is not a word we use in the guard. Someday that Typhon might have to fight a Morgannai in hand-to-hand combat. He must understand his disadvantage on a visceral level before that moment, if he has any chance to prevail."

"So fighting with a Morgannai is part of his training."

"Yes." Bardo turned to face Ryder. "And it will be part of your training."

Ryder quailed as that reality settled in. He glanced over at the ring. A recruit dropped a wad of bloody rags into a pail already half-filled with them. The sight made Ryder's stomach turn. He watched as the recruit returned to the Typhon and helped him to his feet. He could hardly walk.

"What kind of special training do we get before we're paired with a Morgannai?" Ryder asked.

"None."

"Is that your pointer? A warning?"

Bardo laughed. The howl was so loud that every recruit in the gymnasium stared at their captain. "Anton believes you to be one of his brightest. If that's true, you won't ever step into a sparring ring with a Morgannai."

"How can I avoid it if every other recruit is required to do so? Plus, you say they receive no special preparation. What do they do all day while I'm performing my other duties?"

Bardo clapped his shoulder again. "Another good question. It drives home my point. Whatever they do, you won't be present. Being a guard is not a part-time pursuit. We're training elite forces. You'll never be able to match them or meet them in a ring."

"If that's what you believe, why did you ever consent to my training?"

"I didn't consent; I was ordered."

Ryder shifted his feet as the world seemed to tilt around him. He surveyed the gym. Although he refused to stare, Thessar lurked in his peripheral vision. Ryder's head felt light. He had to believe Bardo would never allow the ringmaster to match him with that giant.

Two fresh combatants entered the ring. There were twenty-five recruits in the class, and they were averaging two matches each evening. If he could delay his first time in the ring, maybe he could ferret out some technique to aid him. His heart drummed in his chest as he swallowed his pride. "Can I be called last? Since I'm not an official member of the class?"

Bardo squinted at Ryder. "I'm willing to give you that." He drew his fingers and thumb down his face to hold his chin. "Because you never screamed when I whipped you."

As soon as the training session was dismissed, Ryder hurried across the plaza to the second level of the library. A few zealous scholars remained, but most of the central tables were empty. Ryder strode to the section of the floor that housed the military collection. Beneath the entry arch, he stood perfectly still, absorbing his victory of gained time. There had to be some information within these rooms that could prepare him for hand-to-hand combat with a Morgannai, some technique or insight that would keep him from being annihilated with the first punch.

Isolt's Enchantment

After an exhilarating dawn training session and breakfast, Ryder returned to the attic. He found a single scroll, writing utensils, and a bundle of blank parchment on the table. He opened the scroll and began to read.

✧ ✧ ✧

Frigid air feathered Una's sides. Dark silence engulfed her. Time and space held her spinning body in place.

Barren, she remained a mystery unto herself; the abundant life stirring within her, unreachable. Mostly she slept. Always upon waking, she searched the Void.

Forever it brought her nothing until, once upon time, it did.

✧ ✧ ✧

Una woke to find a giant striding upon her unyielding surface.

Hulking and lame, his footsteps fell heavy and uneven upon her breasts.

"Who goes there?" she cried out.

"It is I, Vulcan, the God of the Dwarves. I seek a home for my people."

"A home? What is this ... home ... you speak of?"

"A place to be living." Vulcan stamped his feet then jumped up and down—hard—upon her belly. "You're quite sturdy and broad."

"What about your people? What kind are you?"

"Masters of the elements. My people are skilled beyond measure in the craft of metal making." The dwarf god bent down to loosen a clod of soil from Una's surface. He rubbed the dirt between his fingers then lifted it to his nose. "We also possess the skill of bringing forth flower and green from rock and stone." Vulcan straightened his crooked body as much as was possible. "Not that our magic would be required to coax the life that dwells within you."

Una sighed as Vulcan's voice thundered through the Void. That someone might want her, desire her, use her, quickened her fervent longing to be known.

As if he knew his words had penetrated Una's center, Vulcan

spoke again. "We can no longer dwell in Azyllai. The gods and goddesses allow us no rest. Night and day they seek us out. Their demands for crowns and swords, boats and baubles made with dwarf magic are ceaseless. I will free my people from their endless claims. Brothers and sisters, father and mother, gods and goddesses they may be; but we must be rid of them." Vulcan spread his arms wide. "You would make a fine home for my people."

For an eternity, Una had craved communion with an other. "Are your people many?" she asked.

Vulcan paced. "From what I sense in the dark, my people will barely touch the fullness of your being, but I must make light to see rightly."

"Light?"

"LIGHT!" bellowed Vulcan. His passion unfurled a need in Una to surrender. He pulled a monstrous pick and shovel from the pack on his back.

Una shuddered. "What will you do with that?"

"Mine your treasures," he growled.

As he tunneled her depths, the dwarf god's grunts and groans filled Una with pleasure. He unearthed a river of silver. When he struck a vein of gold, she shivered. Vulcan thundered his satisfaction. The dwarf god erected a gigantic forge inside her belly.

Una lost count of the days he slaved over the flames that burned and licked her insides. She slept many times before her eyes opened to a million stars gazing down from the heavens. "Brilliant," she murmured.

Vulcan paused to assess his handiwork. Grinning, he acknowledged, "I have surpassed myself."

"Your people—they will come to their new home now?"

"Hardly." Vulcan roared with laughter. "I have only begun." He returned to his fiery forge.

This time when the dwarf god traveled beneath her surface, Una was no longer alone. Now, when she woke from her sleep, the light of a million stars shared her skies. She danced and played with the shining lights as Vulcan toiled for another countless number of days in her belly.

When Vulcan climbed the second time to her surface, the weight of a magnificent silvery orb bent his body in half.

Its gentle glow lit Una's face. Her beauty could be viewed by all.

Vulcan hurled the luminescent ball into the sky. He turned to Una and said, "That is the moon." A single tear dropped from the corner of his eye.

Minding the glowing sphere, Una slept little. First, the moon waned. When she disappeared from the skies, Una's smile vanished with it. But the great round pearl showed herself again, gaining in size and form, until she emblazoned the sky once more with her fullness.

Una whispered to her new friend, "You have created a steady rhythm in my life and awakened me to possibilities."

The day came when the dwarf god crawled for the third time from the depth of Una's belly. Blackened with soot and ash, he labored beneath a magnificent fiery wheel. The wheel flung energy far and wide from the core of its rotation. Vulcan roared, "I name this the Sun."

A great light followed in the wheel's wake, dispelling the darkness.

"What have you done?" Una exclaimed, "I can see all that I am, and I am glorious!"

It took all Vulcan's strength to heave the flaming ball into the heavens where it would dance with the moon, like a lover, across Una's starry skies until the end of time. "The Sun will be recognized as my most marvelous creation."

Indeed it was, for Vulcan's magic created a light which would rise each day from the east, spreading its potent, life-giving force upon Una's fecund belly. Each night it would set in the west, as the moon appeared amidst the sparkle and shine of millions of twinkling stars.

"It's breathtaking," Una murmured. "Can I ever thank you?"

"I will bring my people here. They will nurture you to spectacular abundance. We will all know joy."

Una could not deny the dwarf god.

"I will travel to Azyllai to tell my people the good news," Vulcan said. "I have prepared for them a home where they can live in peace, far from the reach of the gods' and goddesses' mercurial demands."

Una watched Vulcan disappear beyond the boundaries of dark and light, but with the sun, moon, and stars filling her skies, she no longer felt alone.

As the sun warmed her spinning body in the days, and the moon cooled her inner fires at night, life stirred within her.

One day she gave birth to a daughter, beautiful, vivacious and flowing. Una said, "I shall name you Isolt of the Waters, for you have brought with you all the springs, rivers, lakes, and oceans."

Isolt giggled as Una's noble garden blossomed.

When Vulcan returned with his people, the dwarves couldn't

contain their awe.

While the dwarf god had traveled to Azyllai and back, Una had flourished.

Vulcan bowed before her in front of his people. "You have become more than I ever imagined."

"Your gifts have made me magnificent," she said.

All who listened heard the pride in Una's voice.

"My people will make you greater still."

"Is that possible?" Una asked.

With their mystical knowledge of the elements, and their uncanny mastery of the land, it was the destiny of the dwarves to bring forth Una's golden days.

As the dwarves tended Una, three events unfolded in the Whole.

Somewhere between Azyllai and the borders of Una's dark and light, a new world dawned. Born of pure energy and imagination, the Realm of Faerie came into being. Faeries, elves, pixies and brownies drew their first breaths.

The bounty of Isolt's waters overflowed from her mother's world into the Realm of Faerie, binding the worlds in symbiotic union.

In Faerie, the Great White Sea swelled, pouring itself into the mouth of the Nyssalei River, which flowed through Illialei until it filled the bottomless pool of Lake Vivientiana. Forever, there would be a doorway between the worlds.

This was the first thing that happened.

As Isolt's waters spread, the love of all creation grew for her.

Resentment eructed within her mother's depths. Una could never know the flowing grace that was Isolt's essence. It is said she wished her daughter limited and contained, as she was. Envy's long shadow darkened Una's heart.

One day she spoke with Vulcan. "I've never truly paid the debt of gratitude I owe you for all that you've done for me." Her honeyed tone eased the cragged god's impatience.

"Una, you've paid me beyond measure in the happiness of my people. Not only do they thrive on your bounty, but they're free from the foolish demands of the gods and goddesses. You've repaid me well enough. I'll ask no more from you."

Then Una asked this question of Vulcan: "My daughter, Isolt, do you find her attractive?"

"She's a great beauty," he acknowledged.

"She favors you."

Though the dwarf god, heavy and lame, distrusted her words he blushed.

Isolt's Enchantment

"I would offer you her hand in marriage as repayment of my debt."

The dwarf god weighed Una's words. There were many who worshipped Isolt's grace from afar. "She would take me as her husband? She would lay with me?"

Una flinched. "She would be honored to be your queen."

The dwarf god had been crippled by his father at an early age. He was regarded by most as hideous and vulgar. Only the magic in his hands had earned him the right to return to his father's table in the years before he'd abandoned Azyllai once and for all. "I shall be honored then, to take her as my bride," Vulcan answered Una.

An obedient daughter, Isolt yielded to her mother's demands. She stood with the crippled god at the grand wedding ceremony. However, when night fell, she refused to lay with him. She didn't love him.

Her rejection broke Vulcan's sliver of a heart.

Their sterile union, born from a mother's envy, was the second thing that happened in the Whole. It is said it marked the end of Una's glory. For our children are not our possessions, and Isolt was never hers to give away.

Then the third, and most mysterious, development occurred in the Whole.

79

Desire, faith, and ambition amassed into a critical teeming energy within the Realm of Faerie. It seeped through doors and cracks in time and space: Gathering, gathering, gathering; hunting, hunting, hunting new form until: Naked and screaming!

Mortals were born into the Whole.

When mortals learned that Vulcan had created the sun, the moon, and the stars, they bowed in worship. Mortal fathers begged him to lie with their mortal daughters.

Vulcan indulged their adoration. He seeded the children of many mortal women, although unrequited love for Isolt defiled his heart.

One day, a mortal rose to become the first earthly king. Tarquin was firm and powerful, full of passion and life. The first time he laid eyes on Isolt, he fell deeply in love, for there was none more gracious than Isolt of the Waters. Resolved to have her, the earthly king pursued his heart's desire.

She returned his ardor.

The entire world knew of Vulcan's numerous infidelities, and none imagined he would fault Isolt for taking one lover.

The day came when she grew heavy with child.

"You humiliate me before my people by taking a mortal lover. Worms of the earth, these creatures are. You lie with their king and yet refuse me, a god?" As Vulcan thundered, the skies shook.

When Isolt cried, her tears covered Una. "Forgive me," she pleaded with him. "It was my mother's wish that I be your bride. It was never mine. Would you deny me one love? Would you deny me the birth of my child?"

"Una lied to me!" Vulcan raged. "I curse her. I curse her name! Let it be darkened from the annals of time, for it will never be uttered by me or my people again. We will leave your mother to the mortals who crawl like worms upon her belly. They will devour and misuse her. It will be her just payment. But you are my wife. You have betrayed and insulted me. I will see you pay dearly for this, Isolt."

No one had ever seen Vulcan so enraged.

It is said that Una's fear, which came too late for herself and her daughter, erupted in hurricanes and earthquakes, volcanoes and monsoons.

In the chaos, Tarquin died, leaving Isolt abandoned, their defenseless child struggling in her belly.

"We leave for Misgradde tonight." These were Vulcan's decisive words to Isolt. "You'll accompany us. We'll speak no more of this matter." He had already sent a messenger to Quasimi, a mage who lived in the Hidden City.

That night, Vulcan led his people across the borders of time and space into the Realm of Faerie.

True to his word Vulcan never spoke Una's name again.

Abandoned by their god, mortals spun their own stories of creation, renaming their home Eartha, then only Earth.

Humans torment the planet, squandering its abundance. Contamination, deforestation, extinction, pollution, oxygen-depleted dead zones are the gifts they bring.

Some believe the day of her annihilation draws near.

When Vulcan, Isolt, and the dwarves arrived at the shores of the Great White Sea, longboats waited to carry them to Misgradde.

Quasimi greeted Vulcan and his unrepentant bride on the beach of Faerie's northern shores. "The black sparrow came." He addressed Vulcan, who had carved the staff the mage gripped so fervently in his hand. "I must say I was surprised by your summon, although I've long hoped for the opportunity to repay your generosity and skill. There are many who envy my stave," the smooth-tongued mage continued. "The great power you bestowed upon this common branch of oak has made me the wealthiest mage in the Hidden City, my lord. Humbly, I thank you." Quasimi bowed deep before the hulking, lame god while flashing a cruel and crooked smile toward Isolt's growing belly.

Vulcan didn't look at Isolt when he spoke to Quasimi. "This woman is my wife, although the child that grows in her belly isn't mine. It's the seed of a maggot. It will not be born. Do what you must. I never wish to see her face again."

Quasimi bowed deeply before Vulcan once more. "As you wish."

That night, the long boats sailed.

Vulcan left the Realm of Faerie with his people.

None have ever seen him within that country's borders again.

✧ ✧ ✧

Isolt spat at the mage. "You will not touch me."

"You're quite right, my beauty." As Quasimi spoke his features transformed. "I'll not touch you."

A moment later, Isolt swore it was not Quasimi who stood before her but her beloved Tarquin who'd perished in the tempest of her mother's fear.

"My beloved?" Isolt reached her hand toward the illusion.

It grasped her hands and received her tender kiss. Isolt sagged in its arms. Her child's father lived. As she sobbed her elation, the surf rose.

The warm, gravelly voice of Tarquin whispered in her ear, "Come my, love."

Isolt allowed herself to be led from the shore of the Great White Sea. When Tarquin turned in the direction of the mountains, she clung to his fingers with both hands. He was alive. She stumbled behind him. Blinded by tears of jubilation, she mumbled thanks to whatever mystical force had saved her lover, revived him, brought him back from the dead.

Tarquin never ceased walking, nor slowed his pace.

"Can we not rest?" she asked. The terrain was familiar. It was the same mountain pass through which Vulcan had led her earlier. "Where are we going? I won't return to my mother."

"And I wouldn't return you to her," Tarquin promised over his shoulder. He continued to pull Isolt forward. "This new world is ours to share. We'll spend many happy days here, you and I. Our son will grow handsome, strong, and wise. The Realm of Faerie will be his to rule. Have no fear. Your mother is bound to her sphere. She can't reach you now. Come, I've prepared our home. It's close."

Isolt ran to keep up with the ignis fatuu of her beloved mortal king.

Ahead, an enormous marble palace seemed to rise from the

ground. Its polished turrets pierced a darkening sky. Isolt dropped Tarquin's hand. Her elegant feet refused to take another step. The temperature of her body plummeted. A gust of wind threatened to topple her. She wrapped her arms around herself to quell the uncontrollable shivering that possessed her. Tarquin faced her. His face swirled in a spiral. Isolt rubbed her eyes. All this marching. She was exhausted.

He held a key forged from a luminous dark metal in his palm. She let her gaze rise. Her beloved Tarquin stood before her. His shock of blond hair and familiar broad shoulders shushed the foreboding within. She needed rest. Food. Sleep. Water.

"This is our home," he said. "Use the key to unlock the door. Please, so we can live here forever."

With one hand cradling her belly, Isolt reached with the other. The metal was so smooth. So mesmerizing. Clutching the mysterious key, she walked slowly to the palace door. The key practically slipped itself into the lock. As she turned it, she looked back to smile at her beloved king.

He waved her on as she pushed opened the door.

A malignant force gripped her and yanked her within.

Quasimi's black eyes glared from Tarquin's face.

The door slammed shut. The air reverberated. The walls of the palace disintegrated.

Isolt's screams were futile. Buried beneath the highest peak of the Ruadain, black dirt entombed her. No one heard her cries.

Her first thought was of her son. There was no way to save him.

Her next thought was of vengeance. She squeezed the ebon key with raging fingers.

Curiously, the strange dark metal was not an illusion.

Not all the dwarves made the journey to Misgradde. Some traveled no further than Tyrannis and assimilated to life above ground. Some went below ground and dug deep in the bowels of the Ruadain, concealing themselves and their activities in tunnels and mines.

Ryder's heart raced. He imagined Isolt's beauty and her agonizing death—alone and forsaken. The young man comprehended alone. He would have found a way to save her ... and her child.

It's what a hero would have done.

But the Realm of Faerie was far from Idonne, a long journey by ship across the Great White Sea.

He wouldn't be saving anyone anytime soon.

Ryder scratched some notes on one of the blank parchments:

Isolt's Enchantment

The beginnings of the Whole are drowned in sorrow; a promising genesis forever marred by betrayal and injustice.

That evening, the sparring matches riveted Ryder's attention. Two Morgannai were paired for the first bout. By the end of the class, both still staggered around the ring. The match was called a draw. Everyone, including Ryder, cheered. Although he'd been unable to locate any useful information in the library the night before, his obsessive observation had paid off. The Morgannai often used subtle gestures to mislead their opponent. They might curl the fingers of their right hand, as if preparing to make a fist, then pummel with the left. Or they might brace their right leg for a kick with the left, before executing a rapid shuffle that allowed them to lash out with that same right leg. By feinting in a lightening quick manner, they kept their opponent off-balance while minimizing their own injuries.

The technique required speed and precision.

The tale of Hermes' Wand

The next day, a different scroll awaited Ryder on the table. When he rolled open the carved wooden handles, he found a note lodged within:

The events recorded herein are considered of secondary importance to the story of Isolt's Enchantment. However, they merit study. The initial sequence of events occurred before Vulcan led the dwarves from the Realm of Faerie, while the final sequence followed their migration to Misgradde.

Ryder pushed the note aside and began to read.

After Vulcan settled the dwarves in Una's garden, but before he wed Isolt of the Waters, there was little for the god to do. He became restless.

One day a black sparrow lighted on his shoulder. The bird whistled a musical invitation from Quasimi, a mage who dwelled in the Hidden City. "It has been too many days since we have laughed together. Come, visit."

Vulcan counted few as friend. He sent the sparrow ahead of him with this reply: "I will arrive shortly." He would take Quasimi a gift. Something to delight him.

The dwarf god possessed as much skill over wood as he did over metal. He cut a branch from a towering white oak.

The spirit of the tree emerged. Crimson stained her fingers. She staunched the flow of blood from a gash in her side. "You bereave me with no consideration?"

Vulcan fumbled for words. His glance darted between the wood in his hand and the tree spirit's wound. "I didn't know you were alive."

"Your lack of awareness is apparent."

He held out the branch, to return it to her.

"No. It is like a child. Once born it cannot re-enter the womb. But know this: It will retain memory of the roots that birthed it."

"I meant to use it for a gift."

"Do with it what you will, but don't steal from me again."

"And your wound?"

"It will heal in time." The tree spirit re-entered the white oak.

Hoping to appease her outrage, the abashed god whittled and scraped the wood with care. He risked a glance at the oak when he was finished.

The tree remained silent.

Vulcan admired the smooth and slender staff in his hands. The pale wood required no adornment. And yet, he desired his gift to be impressive. He called upon his cousin, Hermes. "Perhaps you could endow the rod with some contrary magic?"

The nimble messenger god hefted the staff. "You could crack a head with this."

Vulcan flinched when his cousin smashed it against the stout trunk of a tree. When Hermes threw the rod to the ground and jumped upon it with both feet, Vulcan shouted, "Enough!"

The rod remained whole and unmarred. "It's indestructible," Hermes said.

"Don't test it with fire," Vulcan warned.

The young god sniffed. "Not indestructible?"

Vulcan grabbed the stick. "That is precisely why I left Azyllai.

You gods are impossible to please!"

"Are those flames spouting from your ears, dear cousin?"

"Why must the staff be indestructible for you to be impressed with its artistry?"

Hermes chuckled. "But you're the God of the Forge. What better trick than to protect wood from fire?"

"Forget that I asked for your help!" Vulcan stormed off.

Hermes, much lighter on his feet, soon matched the dwarf god's stride. "I have an idea."

The ground shook with Vulcan's every step.

"To catch someone in a lie without accusation, that would be a playful, not to mention, useful trick," Hermes teased. "Would it not?"

Vulcan halted his crashing gait through the woods.

The angelic young god held out his hand. "To reveal the truth is pleasurable, to disguise it more so. But to disguise the ability to reveal the truth? How amusing!" He curled his fingers around the rod. He chanted over the wood, his spell sounding more like a rush of soft wind than words. When he finished, he returned the staff to Vulcan. "Speak the truth, and the rod will maintain its unremarkable appearance. However, utter one false word with the staff in hand, and light will shoot from the wood in blazing indictment."

"A lie detector in disguise," Vulcan mused. It would indeed be an entertaining gift for a mage living in a city of mages and sorcerers. "Many thanks." He clapped Hermes on the shoulder.

The slight god buckled under the force of the gesture.

Vulcan caught him before he reached the ground.

Righted, Hermes fluttered his enormous snow-white wings. "Your gentle touch is sorely missed in Azyllai."

"They mourn the lack of jewels and baubles. That is all."

Hermes' eyes twinkled as his feet left the ground. "Any message for your father?"

Vulcan gripped the wand. "Send my love."

Both gods laughed as a whirlwind of light spiraled around them.

✧ ✧ ✧

Inhabiting neither time nor space, the Hidden City moves throughout the Whole as a vapor passes across the sky. It is to the Whole as dreams are to the individual, existing—and yet, not. A mystery whose purpose has not yet been revealed, few enter the city, and few who dwell there ever leave, although there is a gate.

✧ ✧ ✧

Vulcan stood before the filigree portal—its height and width intimidating even to a god!—with his fingers tight upon the wand.

The gatekeeper stared with bulging yellow eyes while the talons of his beastly lower body clenched and unclenched the ledge of the marble pedestal upon which he crouched. "You must answer a riddle to gain entry."

The dwarf god detested word games.

A swollen gray tongue flicked the creature's bloated lips. "What gives wings but never flies, gives warmth without a fire, and receives no tomb on the day it dies?"

"Perhaps we could strike a bargain," Vulcan said.

The gatekeeper's barbed ears pricked up. "What did it say?"

Vulcan thrust his walking stick at the half-man, half-beast. "Hold this while I ask you three questions. Answer one of them with a lie. When we're done, if I can tell you which answer was the lie, then you will let me pass."

The creature grasped the stick with long talons. His eyes narrowed while he examined it with exaggerated scrutiny. "What curious game does it play?" he murmured, before leaning against the rod and returning his cloudy gaze to the petitioner before him. "Ask your question, but if you lose, I keep this piece of wood."

Vulcan agreed. "What is your name?"

"Iro."

The wand remained dull.

"What is the answer to the riddle you asked me?"

The gatekeeper narrowed his eyes. "True love."

The wand cast no light.

Vulcan grunted. "Will you give me passage if I win our game?"

The gate keeper snickered. "Of course."

Beams of light emanated from the wand.

Iro dropped the wood as if it had charred his puckered hand. "What kind of trick is this?"

"Shedding light upon the darkness of deceit," Vulcan murmured as he bent to retrieve Hermes' Wand. "You didn't intend to hold to our agreement. You answered my third question with a lie. But the answer to your riddle is *true love*. So you must allow me passage."

Iro snarled, exposing a row of vicious blackened teeth. Nevertheless, he opened the Hidden City's gate to grant the stranger entry.

Vulcan entered the opulent city of magic. His gaze flitted from one spectacular scene to the next. Intricate mosaics of gold and gemstones paved streets along which the most virile men and sublime women passed. They rode magnificent horses, in luxurious carriages, on commandeered dragons; or danced with abandon, their feet barely grazing the ground.

After drinking in enough amazing sights to put himself in a stupor, the dwarf god went in search of his friend.

Quasimi's delight with the wand satisfied Vulcan immensely. The mage invited his guest to share his table. They ate and drank until neither god nor mage could manage a single bite more.

The gaming houses called. It was time to test the wand.

Every player in the Hidden City used magic, so there could be no accusations of foul play with the wand's power; its only limitation was that a certain strategic manipulation was required to reap the wand's truth-telling benefit: The card player had to have the device firmly in hand for truth or lie to be detected.

Quasimi reveled in the game, calculating when the most gold was at risk. At these times, the mage created a distraction or interruption with the staff designed to peak his opponent's interest in it. Once he gave Hermes' Wand over to the competition, the mage would pose a casual question regarding the player's hand.

Gold overflowed his and Vulcan's pockets as the pair jigged their way home.

The next day, the two friends toasted their bright futures. With the magic of Hermes' Wand, Quasimi would become the wealthiest mage in the Hidden City, and Vulcan was deeply pleased with the life he'd created for himself and his people upon Una's breasts and belly.

Soon after Vulcan returned to Una, she gave the dwarf god her daughter's hand in marriage under false pretense.

Despite her deceit, peace reigned until Isolt fell in love with the mortal king, Tarquin, and conceived a child.

When Una's tempests drowned the great white oak from which Hermes' Wand was hewn, the wood of the wand felt the loss, as if its mother had been murdered.

It yearned to find a way home.

One night, Quasimi stayed up late playing cards with the Huron, Erick of Egonne. Although Quasimi held a weak hand, he believed he could win with the aid of his stave. The mage made a great show of stamping the stick against the ground.

"Do you always bang your staff so?" Erick asked. "I'm surprised the thing doesn't break."

"My apologies." Quasimi thrust the wand in the knight's direction.

Erick's fingers circled the wood. "It's more substantial than it appears. No wonder your harsh treatment leaves no mark upon it."

"You must have all the high cards," Quasimi said.

The Huron's hand lay face-down on the table. He still held the staff, examining it. "What? No."

Hermes' Wand remained dull.

A reckless impulse seized Quasimi. He bet all the gold on the table.

Erick's eyebrows rose. He called the bet.

They showed their cards.

Quasimi's heart plunged. The wand had played trickster and turned against him. He could never trust the wood again. "Keep the useless thing." He shoved Erick's winnings across his table with such force that coins spun from the table and rolled in all directions. The mage stalked from the gaming hall without a backward glance.

A few days later, Quasimi found the first grey hair in his jet black beard.

Erick of Egonne came to love the wand for its simple beauty. Although he never discovered the wand's secret power, he carried the stave with him always. To the Huron knight, the wand was an invincible staff. He used it as a weapon.

The knight sailed from port to port in search of adventure. In Typhos, he heard tales of a rogue dragon tormenting the population of the Black Magic Islands. Erick's campaign against the dragon failed. The beast chased the knight from the island, threatening to turn Hermes' Wand into kindling.

The urge to visit Faerie seized the knight. He booked passage to a bustling port in the valley. In those days, a row of gambling houses lined the Nyssalei River. Erick drank blackberry wine, smoked woodvine, and tested his luck at them all. When he'd spent the last of Quasimi's gold, he curled beneath a gigantic banyan tree, wrapped himself in his coat, and drifted off to sleep.

The wand—so close to home—bided its time beside him.

A siren came across Erick in the depth of the night. She found his strong jaw and golden-red whiskers appealing. Her melancholy song called him to the river. As she took him in her embrace, the wand slipped from his fingers and floated away.

Many days later, Erick woke as if from a dream, both wand and siren gone.

The wand was recovered on the shores of the Nyssalei by a curious young wood elf named Aldous. Sensing the power inherent in the staff, he determined to unravel its mysteries. When the elf became Head Librarian of the Cathedral Palace Grand Library, he took the walking stick with him.

Eventually, Aldous came across some scribblings about a magical staff with the ability to discern the truth. He tested the wand. The elf kept his discovery to himself and hid the wand in the back of a simple cabinet.

One day its magic might be useful.

Ryder closed the scroll.

He wondered if Hermes' Wand remained imprisoned in a cabinet in the Cathedral Palace. The name Aldous seemed familiar to him. Anton gathered information from contacts throughout the enchanted world, perhaps the priest had communicated with the wood elf.

Ryder made a note to ask his mentor about it before adding a timeline to the parchment he'd scribbled upon the day before.

That night after class, Ryder searched for an isolated courtyard to practice what he'd learned from watching the Morgannai fight. He began his session with the basic drills he'd learned over the past two mornings: two-handed body lifts and presses; horizontal holds; wide-stride paces; and angled-leg dips. When he'd exhausted his repertoire, he punched the air as he bounced around the dirt square on the balls of his feet, mimicking the fighters when they first entered the ring. The exertion quieted his mind and invigorated his body, even though it was late in the day.

He was ready to begin experimenting. He partially curled the fingers of his left hand then formed a fist with his right. It was hard to resist completing the left fist. He forced himself to slow down and create a rhythm. After what seemed like a thousand efforts, the movement began to feel more fluid. However, as soon as he increased the speed of the movement, it was again difficult to resist closing his left fist. He slowed down again. Stubbornly, he persisted; slowing down, speeding up, slowing down, speeding up —until he could perform the movement quickly.

By the time he reached his new quarters—the box of a room assigned to all first-level priests—dawn was only a few hours away.

Ryder didn't care. He'd achieved something to build on.

The tale of Haff and Gweff

Ryder's next day's work was a slim, bound volume. He wasted no time immersing himself in its pages.

The dwarves Haff and Gweff ended their day sweaty, dirty, cold, and tired.

"Nothing but drops of water to drink and none to bathe in," said Gweff.

"Prefer to be spineless in Misgradde?" Haff griped.

The dwarves rested back-to-back in a pitch black cave.

"Not saying that at all. What I'm saying is we've got to find another stream. This one has dried up." Gweff felt around for a butt of wax. Using one of the few matches in the bottom of his jacket pocket, he lit the stump.

"In the morning, then. What have we got for dinner?" Haff growled.

"Rats, bugs, and some old dried snake meat is about all."

"What I wouldn't give for a nice piece of fresh fish frying on a grill."

"With some nice charred greens, boiled potatoes, and ice cold bitters. That's the way to end a long—"

"Shhhhhh," Haff interrupted his friend.

"What?"

"Listen."

Water dripped from the cave's ceiling, splashing dully against the dirt floor.

"Can you hear that?" Haff whispered.

"What's the big fuss?" Gweff scowled. "It's not like you've never heard water drops before."

"Shut up and listen. Off in the distance. Someone's singing."

A faint song drifted through the tunnels. "I hear it," Gweff whispered.

"It's the most beautiful sound I've ever heard," said Haff.

"It's sad is what it is."

Haff stood up. "I'm going to go find whoever is singing that song."

"How are you gonna do that?" Gweff remained hunkered on the ground. "With all the tunnels we've made, you'll be lost for days."

Haff ignored him. "It's her," he said. "I can feel it in my bones."

"What do you mean it's *her*?"

"It's Isolt."

"We've been trying to track her down all these years and nothing." Gweff shook his head. "Now you think she's serenading you?"

"She mourns for her child."

"Mind you," said Gweff, "no need to romanticize that child. It was half mortal."

"If we help her, she'll be bound to us. She'll have to grant us our heart's deepest wish."

"I'm not sure you've got a heart," Gweff mumbled beneath his breath.

Haff snarled back, "I've got one."

"Then you best be knowing what's deep inside it before you totter off to make deals with the likes of her. That's all I'm saying."

"I know what I want," Haff snapped.

"Bewitched is what you are."

"Bewitched?" Haff fumed. "What have we been up to down here, never seeing the light of day and trusting those damned trolls to bring us food and wood?" Haff kicked a log across the cave. "Searching for Isolt. That's what. Well, that's her singing down the hall. Are you gonna go all chicken-livered on me now?"

"We've never been to Misgradde," Gweff wheedled. "It might be all right."

"Misgradde," Haff frothed the name in disgust. "I didn't follow the puppet master to Misgradde because I'm not made of wood." He waved his hands then each leg. "Do you see any strings on me? No, you don't, because Una's land belongs to us, not to the mortals bent on her destruction. Isolt's our ticket home."

"What if she's angry?" Gweff asked.

"She won't be angry with us." Haff jabbed his finger against his chest and then against his friend's.

"Fine." Gweff held the candle above his head. "You lead the way."

Haff entered the maze of tunnels they'd dug over the centuries. Gweff followed his friend down the darkened path, shivering when the song grew louder.

"It's lovely," Haff whispered.

"Aye. Just gorgeous if your taste runs to broken hearts."

They walked a hundred more feet and then hit a wall. Haff pressed his ear against the rock, tapping it with his fingers. "It's hollow. She's in there. I'm sure of it."

Gweff handed Haff the melting candle, then pulled a small pickaxe from his belt. His friend wasn't going to quit until he found out what was on the other side. "Out of my way. I'll knock it down."

Other than holding the stub of wax, Haff stood idle for the better part of an hour while Gweff sweated and puffed. When there was a space large enough for both of them to wiggle through, Haff pushed his friend through the hole. When Gweff landed safely, Haff handed the greasy, flickering light into the pitch black before squeezing through himself. His feet hit the dirt beside Gweff.

The singing stopped.

They stood at the edge of a cavernous room. A huge dirt mound occupied its center. The sound of running water whispered from a distance. Cautiously, they approached the mound.

"Ouch!"

It was Gweff's turn to, "Shhhhhh!"

Haff whispered in a loud voice, "I've stepped on something hard. Bring that light over here. I want to see what it is."

Gweff tiptoed to where Haff was bent over, running his fingers across the ground. When the circle of light from the candle embraced Haff, something glinted on the floor next to his feet.

"Aha!"

"What is it?" Gweff kept his voice low as he sidled up to his friend.

"It's a key. Look at this metal. I've never seen anything like it."

Gweff lifted the key from Haff's palm.

"Give that back to me. I found it!" Haff barked.

"Or what?" Gweff snapped back.

"Who goes there?" A ghostly voice rippled through the darkness. "Who steals my key?"

Haff's and Gweff's eyes popped wide. Gweff dropped the key as he whirled to face the disembodied voice. Behind him, Haff squatted to pick it up. He slipped the key in his pocket.

"Who goes there?"

"It is Haff, the d-dwarf," Haff stuttered, "and m-my companion

G-g-g–"

Gweff shoved him aside. Stepping forward, he kneeled. "Gweff, the dwarf, at your service, milady."

Haff shoved Gweff aside. "It was my idea to find you!"

"And why do you seek me when no one else does?"

"You'll be bound to us if we end your enchantment," Haff said.

Gweff scowled in the candlelight. Silent and stooping, he gave Haff a good strong kick in the ass.

Haff flew forward and landed face down with a mouthful of dirt.

Gweff addressed the mound. "We wish things to be as they once were–before mortals walked upon Una's body, when the noble garden bloomed, and Isolt's grace was the crowning glory of us all."

Haff crawled up onto his knees. "So now we have a poet in our midst." He got to his feet and made a running leap, landing on Gweff's back with his arms around his friend's throat.

The force sent them both sprawling. Rolling across the packed dirt, they clawed at each other's eyes and showered one another with stone fists.

"Do not fight in my presence!" Isolt's voice boomed.

Haff and Gweff froze.

When he recovered his breath, Haff glared at Gweff. "Don't

you screw this up for us."

Wisps of sorrow encircled them. A musical moaning, Isolt's song swelled from the depths into an ethereal, heartbreaking lament. Words formed, slow, drawn out, each plaintive syllable extended upon echoing notes:

Loveless—childless—tearless—

I endure.

The—darkest—flame—of—vengeance—

I burn.

Haff gulped. "Lady Isolt, we're dwarves. We can fire magical objects with the power to set you free." The dwarf made a sweeping bow.

"I need to act far beyond the Ruadain. Do you have dwarfish magic for that?"

Gweff tugged on Haff's jacket, but Haff knocked his hand away. "We're masters of element and fire. We've made many objects that have pleased the gods and goddesses of Azyllai."

"There is no time to waste. Bring me what I need. Then I will see what I can do for you."

"Yes, milady, we'll return as soon as our work is done." Haff grabbed Gweff by the ear, pulling him back toward the hole in the wall.

When Gweff sought to speak again, Haff clamped his hand over Gweff's mouth. Gweff bit down hard.

"Ow!" Haff choked Gweff's neck, hugging his friend's back against his chest. He shoved his backside through the hole in the wall, pulling Gweff with him. "Let go of my fingers," he hissed.

"Geth dem out of my mouff!" Gweff squirmed against his friend's stranglehold.

"We're stuck."

Gweff butted Haff with the back of his head. His blow forced both their upper bodies through the gap they were wedged in. Their legs flipped over their heads as they crashed into the adjoining tunnel in a tangled heap.

"Now what?" Gweff untwisted himself. He crept toward the tiny spot of orange-red flickering in the darkness. Being careful not to burn his fingers, he reached for the warm wax and re-lit the stub.

Haff pulled a small, dark object from his pocket. "Now we go to work. Just like the lady said."

"You stole her key?"

"It can open a passageway between our plane and the Void." Haff turned the ebon key over and over in his hand. "It needs to be recast."

"She'll need a portal," Gweff said. "The last vein of silver we struck was of high quality. I'll use it to craft a shield—or broad dish. Without a door to unlock, any new key you forge will be useless."

Obsessed with the metal in his hand, Haff scarcely heard his friend.

For the next several months, the two dwarves toiled night and day at their forges. When Haff finished first, his laughter echoed through the tunnels.

Curious to see his friend's handiwork, Gweff stopped his own. Taking his axe, he followed the winding maze to his friend's workshop. Outside Haff's forge, Gweff gasped.

An enormous, fur-covered beast with hideous fangs attacked his friend.

Gweff charged into the fiery workshop, axe swung high above his head. He hacked and hacked. By the time he realized there was no beast—only ghastly shadows cast by a wicked fire—his lifelong friend lay dead in his arms.

Tears streamed down Gweff's face as he cradled Haff's bloody head. "I'm so sorry, my dear friend. I'm so, so sorry." He couldn't stop weeping.

Days later, thirst woke him. The fire had died out. Gweff felt the cold hardness of Haff's body against his. A few feet away, a slim blue light shimmered. Gweff crawled toward it. His fingers touched a fine blade.

Haff had forged a masterpiece.

Running his finger along its length, Gweff sought the hilt. He gripped the handle, using the sturdy blade to help him stand. Light as a feather, the blade held his weight.

Gweff staggered back through the tunnels to his workshop. He rekindled his forge. In the light of the fire, he considered the sword. He didn't recognize the luminescent blue metal. "Where did Haff mine it?" he wondered out loud.

The blade's hilt was crafted from the dark metal of Isolt's key. A small, magnificent ruby adorned its burnished center.

Gweff held the sword high, then sliced air. Haff had crafted the blade to perfection.

"I shall name you Koldis, for you shall release Isolt of the Waters from her eternal bondage." Gweff spoke the words to awaken the magic Haff had instilled in the sword.

He balanced Koldis against the dirt wall of the cave and threw a log upon the fire of his forge. Determined to best Haff's sword, he hummed as he worked. Twelve days later he held in his hands an exquisite basin, forged from the finest silver.

One-and-a-half feet in circumference, it could stand upright upon any pedestal or patch of ground. Brilliant gemstones encrusted its fluted edges. A shallow, spherical indentation marked the deepest point of the basin's center.

"I shall name you Ormrun, for you are suffused with the serpent's secret wisdom of death and rebirth. Filled with mystical waters from the Great White Sea, you will serve as Isolt's eye. Through your vision, Isolt shall seek the perfect vessel for reincarnation. When the time comes, Koldis will pierce your center, unlocking the door through which Isolt shall pass into the Whole, breathing and alive. She'll be free to take vengeance upon those who have held her captive and stolen the life of her unborn child."

At the thought of Isolt's release, Gweff wept bitterly. His return to Una would be joyless without Haff's companionship.

Gweff allowed himself one night's rest before he journeyed back to Isolt's cavern.

"Who goes there?" Isolt's hearing was keen.

"It is I, Gweff, your humble servant."

"You claim to be my humble servant, yet your deepest desire would extract a high price were I to accept the gifts you bring me. Tell me, where is your friend? Why do you return alone?"

"A tragic accident occurred."

"Tragic accident or the fulfillment of a heart's dark desire?"

"No ... I mean ... yes. It was an accident."

"In the years I've lain beneath the Ruadain, I've learned there is much which is evil in the hearts of all creatures. Given the right circumstances, it will awaken."

Gweff shivered. He'd never wished his friend dead.

"What have you brought me?" Isolt commanded.

"A basin named Ormrun and a blade named Koldis." As Gweff placed the magical objects on the edge of Isolt's mound, he doubted the wisdom of doing so.

"Trinkets are useless to me," Isolt sulked.

"These are not decorative items milady." Gweff picked up the bowl. "To return to our plane, your essence must re-incarnate. That will require a body–a vessel. As a water elemental, you're aware the waters of the Great White Sea have supernatural power?"

"Of course!"

"Ormrun is a portal. When filled with water from the Great

White Sea, the basin will be as an eye. Your sight will be able to roam the enchanted and mortal worlds. You'll be able to seek and choose a vessel of incarnation." If he had any courage, he'd run.

"How will I accomplish this when I can no longer reach Faerie's shore to activate the bowl's power?" Isolt's bodiless voice exuded a haze which muddled his thoughts.

"You'll need a servant." The sound of a quavering voice echoed in the chamber, Gweff touched his lower lip. The voice was his. "I-I-I will serve you and fill the bowl with water from the Great White Sea." Despite his desire to withhold the secret magic imbued in the basin and sword, he continued to speak. "Once you have chosen your vessel, they must draw close to the basin." He tried to stop offering instructions, but found that he couldn't. "I will plunge Koldis through Ormrun's center. The Void will open, and you will be reborn to the Whole."

"How can I trust you? It was your god who cast me beneath the mountains." Isolt's anger ricocheted off the cavern's walls.

Gweff ducked. The urge to crawl snaked up his spine. "M' lady —Isolt—Vulcan abandoned not only you, but Una's noble garden as well. He left our home to the mortals who cannot tend it. I vow no allegiance to him." His words, meant to placate her, tasted as salt on his tongue. A dry heave caught in his throat.

"You betray your god, yet have the gall to stand before me, asking that I trust you?"

The dwarf continued his charade. He almost convinced himself of his sincerity. "My good friend has given his life, and I have created my greatest work. These gifts I present you are powerful. No other could have rendered them. I am here to serve you."

Gweff searched for the tunnel's black mouth. The one that had spit him out, moments ago, with such naive hope.

Freeing Isolt had been Haff's dream. Never his. Forsaking their foolish mission now would be a relief. He slid his foot to the left.

"Fill Ormrun with water from the Great White Sea." Isolt commanded. "But mark my words: I'll be bound to the one who sets me free, not simply to the craftsman."

To hide his changing heart, Gweff bowed so deeply his forehead scraped the ground.

A vibration from deep in the mountain shook the huge pile of dirt in the middle of the cavern.

The dwarf exaggerated his false display. "I'll serve you milady. It will be my honor to serve you." She didn't deserve the sword and basin. By some mysterious power, her hand—her desire—had guided Haff's death.

Gweff secured Ormrun across his chest with one arm. He lifted

Koldis from the ground. He nodded and bowed as he back-stepped his way out of the cavern.

When he was beyond Isolt's eerie grasp, he turned and ran.

It was many days before Gweff stumbled upon a shaft of light, filtering through a fissure large enough for him to squeeze through. Blinded by sunshine, he collapsed, dropping Ormrun and Koldis beside him.

Isolt lived? In some disembodied form in the Void?

Ryder scratched some notes on a parchment. He froze.

The sword—Koldis. It was the blade in the archives. The one displayed in the heart of the library's labyrinthine halls.

The young scholar rose from the bench to pace the long, narrow room.

The blade had been forged in the Realm of Faerie.

He paused to gaze out the window. Beyond the visible golden roofs, the Great White Sea beat Idonne's rocky shoreline.

Who had brought the blade here? And where was its counterpart now, the basin—Ormrun?

Ryder lived for his two classes with the guard. The early morning drills strengthened his spirit as much as his body, and his focused awareness during the sparring classes increased his alertness to all his surroundings. He'd often walk through the streets of the citadel and the halls of the library in a daze, daydreaming about visiting the Hidden City or imagining a life in the Realm of Faerie. Now, when he moved through his days, he was attuned to the details of his environment.

Although it robbed him of much-needed sleep, Ryder continued his solo training sessions at night. He'd begin each one tired and worn out, but as he gave himself to the repetitive movements, he would become energized. He always stayed up later than he intended.

"You look exhausted," Shilda said.

Twice every moon cycle the order and the guard recessed, allowing the priests and students, guard members and recruits, to spend their days as they wished. Garrick and his wife, Shilda, had made the day-long trip from their home to spend these afternoons with Ryder for as long as he could remember.

"I've missed our morning visits," Garrick said.

Before he'd begun his training, Ryder had often stopped by the grain pantry for a brief exchange with the baker before breakfast.

"I've begun training with the guard," Ryder exclaimed.

A shadow crossed Shilda's sky-blue eyes like a fast-moving cloud.

"How is that going?" Garrick asked.

"I'm limited to two classes, but it fulfills me in a way that studying never has."

"What do you mean?" Shilda asked.

"I feel like I've been following instructions my entire life, doing whatever was asked of me. But these drills and sparring sessions spark something deeper within me. I feel more alive every day. In fact, it's harder and harder for me to sit still. Do you feel like walking?" Ryder asked. They sat in the visitor's plaza beyond the citadel gates. It wasn't uncommon for the three to spend an entire afternoon settled on the benches in conversation. But today, Ryder longed to explore.

Garrick and Shilda exchanged glances. "Do you want to go to the market?"

"No, I'd like to visit the Temple of Delphinus."

"That's a lovely idea," Shilda said. "Have you ever been?"

"No," Ryder admitted.

Shilda rose before Garrick could respond. "If we leave now, we can arrive in time for the choir's twilight performance."

Idonne was a giant sandbox. An enormous desert flattened the countries central planes. Garrick and Shilda lived on the country's eastern border. As a healer, Shilda was able to cultivate a greater variety of plants and herbs in the rich mix of clay and sand that existed in the swathe of land at the bottom of the mountains.

The citadel dominated a large block of Idonne's southwest quadrant. Irrigation was required for the sparse fruit trees and rare blossoming plants that existed in its walls. To the north, east, and west, sand dunes cradled the citadel's perimeter. But to the south, the sand gave way to increasingly rocky terrain.

The Temple of Delphinus was built atop a stony promontory whose southernmost tip jutted out across the Great White Sea. Although the road between the citadel and temple was well-traveled, Ryder had never had the desire to visit the shrine before.

Garrick and Shilda listened as Ryder spoke about his training. He hadn't meant to confide so much, but he became more and more animated as they walked. He confessed his need to make a decent showing of his first match.

Although they offered no words of discouragement, Ryder sensed Garrick and Shilda's concern. At one point, he stood in front of Shilda and reached for her hands. "I'll be fine."

She squeezed his hands in return. "Of course you will be." Her faint smile belied her verbal assurance, but it was too late for Ryder to reconsider his blind determination.

When they reached the temple, the choir was lining up on the broad stone stairway in front of the cathedral. A large audience gathered before them. A soloist with an angelic voice opened the first hymn. Ryder stilled. When the voices of the choir joined the song like a flock of birds in tandem flight, his heart soared. As the ethereal performance continued, an unfamiliar yearning simultaneously burst forth and contracted in his chest. He longed to both remember and forget. What? Something wavered at the edges of his mind. It plucked at the edges of his consciousness. He chased the wisps of a memory, but they were so faint.

Ryder remained silent during the lengthy hike back to the citadel. It was dark by the time Garrick and Shilda said farewell at the citadel gate.

That night, Ryder felt drained. He went straight to bed and fell into a deep sleep. The dream fragments that whispered away when he woke the following morning left both sorrow and elation in their wake.

Josefina and the Magic Basin

The next day, when Ryder arrived in the attic, several pieces of loose parchment had been left on the table.

Upon holding the silver bowl with the bejeweled rim in her hands, Josefina desired it. The muannaye barely listened to the dwarf's ravings as she ran her finger across the diamonds, emeralds, sapphires, and single ruby. Something within her awoke at the feel of the unyielding gemstones.

The dwarf fidgeted, bounced on his toes, and scratched his

head. He looked over his shoulder as if some evil chased him. What registered with Josefina was his desperation to leave the Realm of Faerie. He planned to sail for Misgradde.

There was nothing strange about that. A huge population of dwarves dwelled in that country, and she had no doubt the fare was expensive.

The dwarf traveled with a caravan of peddlers. They murmured among themselves that the price the dwarf demanded for the bowl was too high. No one would pay gold for a bowl, no matter how beautiful it was. Their horses grew restless.

Josefina ignored them, and without even bargaining, paid the exorbitant sum the dwarf requested.

He received the coins with an unsteady hand. "I have something else that might suit you." He hurried to one of the carts, dug beneath a tarp, and returned with a second package wrapped in filthy cloth. "It's a sword as beautiful as the bowl." He thrust it toward her as if his sole desire in the Whole was to rid himself of it.

The thing repelled Josefina. She refused to touch it. "The basin will do."

The dwarf's eyes shrank as he stepped away from her. He assessed her with greater care. "Never fill the bowl with water from the Great White Sea."

Josefina waved her long hand and smiled—to humor him. He was obviously mad.

The moment the dwarf and his caravan disappeared over the horizon, a dry wind rose from the basin's depths. Had she imagined it? Josefina studied her reflection, distorted by the divot in the basin's center. Strands of black hair, framing her face, stirred in a hot breeze. She raised her head. The world around her was quiet.

"Regina, did you feel that?"

Her daughter waited with crossed arms on the side of the road. "What?" She cared little for her mother's interests and concerns.

Regina's father was a sorcerer from Kyrakkos. Soon after Josefina had given birth to a son, he'd taken the boy and left Faerie. Regina blamed her mother for her father's abandonment.

Josefina ran the back of her fingers against her cheek. Her skin felt warm. "That hot gust?"

Regina offered pursed lips and an impatient shake of her head.

When Josefina returned her gaze to the bowl, the air remained still. With reluctance she wrapped the basin with the same thick cloth the dwarf had used to cover it. She re-tied the twine to create a handle. Despite its size, the bowl was light and easy to carry.

At night, Josefina slept with her hand resting upon the bulky package. Her dreams became vivid and troublesome. She kicked and moaned, often waking her daughter. Regina said nothing, only moved her pallet farther away.

The pair veered from their original path and found themselves before the roar of the Great White Sea. Josefina quickened her pace. Regina dawdled.

Josefina knelt before the tide. She scooped up sea water with both hands and poured it into the bowl. When it was full, she carried the full basin back toward the beach, away from the waves.

An aching melody drifted above the roar of the ocean. Its forlorn sound sliced opened Josefina's heart. The bitter loss of her son poured out. She bowed her neck and peered more closely into the basin. The song became louder and more anguished. The melody rose higher and higher, fluttering around the muannaye like a wounded bird.

A black flame unfurled beneath the water's surface. A magnificent illusion? Although it felt like her heart would shatter into infinite pieces, Josefina couldn't avert her gaze.

The bowl grew warm to the touch. Josefina remained mesmerized. A promise rose from its depths, annihilation of both pain and joy.

Exquisite emptiness.

Josefina gazed into the Void.

Penetrating heat burned her palms. It shocked her from her trance. She couldn't let go of the bowl.

The water within bubbled and steamed. A towering inferno exploded.

Regina's mouth hung open. Not trusting what she saw, she advanced as if in a nightmare. The rush of the fire and crackle of the flames was real, so were her mother's piercing cries. When Regina crossed her hands to shield her face, heat blistered her forearms.

The fire snuffed out as quickly as it had erupted.

Regina took one ginger step after another.

Beside the unscathed silver basin her mother's bones lay, bleached white and dry as driftwood.

Tears rolled down Regina's cheeks as she gathered them, along with the deadly artifact. She wrapped everything in the same cloth and twine Josefina had used to carry the hateful thing across Faerie.

At night, Regina placed the bundle as far away from her as she dared. When she thought she heard a sad melody, or the moaning of a mother who had lost her son, Regina covered her ears or sang loud songs to drown out the wailing.

When she reached the edge of the Balyudor–Faerie's wild woods—she dug a deep pit near a sapling yew. Her body shook with rage and regret as she tore into the dirt. She wiped her snotty nose and burning eyes with grimy hands. Too late, her love for her mother bloomed.

Regina never spoke of the bowl, or the dwarf, or what she'd witnessed. She couldn't bear to. Whenever anyone asked after Josefina, she lied. She told them her mother's lover, the great black sorcerer from Kyrakkos, had finally sent for the ones he'd left behind. But Regina preferred to remain in Faerie, she said. It was her home.

Regina's unexpected grief over her mother's death scored some invisible wound in Ryder's heart. Her story compounded the strange wave of emotion that had flooded him since he'd heard the temple choir. Through the years, Ryder had pushed away all questions about the female who'd given birth to him. She hadn't wanted him, or cared to raise him. The rejection was so deep, the hole so black, he kept his distance lest the wound engulfed him.

"The dwarf artifacts are powerful," Anton's voice startled

Ryder.

"I didn't hear you enter."

"You were engrossed in your work."

Ryder shuffled the parchment. "The potency you spoke of, it is the force that reached through the bowl and killed the muannaye?"

Anton settled on the bench beside Ryder. "I think not. I think the force that killed Josefina was Isolt's rage."

"But you spoke of another energy gathering in the Void."

"Indeed. There is still much to read. The stories interest you?"

"None of the scrolls are signed. Who wrote them?"

"I'm not the original author, but they're my life work. It's taken years to piece together these documents from fragments documented by scholars who are more perceptive than I." He sighed. "Scholars who have long since passed. That is why it's so imperative for you to continue the work. I no longer have time to devote to detailed investigations."

"How did you come by the sword?"

Anton stroked his beard. "You remember it?"

Three thin, white scars across Ryder's back promised he would never forget it. "Yes."

"The Order was presented with the opportunity to purchase it, and did so."

"Is it safe here?"

"That is not your concern."

The admonishment chafed. "What is my concern?"

"The completion of the tasks you've been assigned. Is that so difficult?"

Anton's imperious manner was becoming harder and harder for Ryder to bear. However, if he released his pent-up resentment directly, he risked losing the one thing that mattered to him most —the opportunity to train with the guard.

Ryder marched across the citadel to the empty courtyard where he practiced most nights. He intended to burn up his swallowed words with an exhaustive round of drills before sunset.

A shadow fell across the sandy ground.

Ryder, executing a horizontal hold, glanced up.

Thessar's bulk towered over him.

"Hah!" the giant guffawed. He raised his foot to let it rest in the middle of Ryder's back.

Ryder imagined his body as a wood plank. He clenched his teeth and every muscle in his body.

Thessar gradually exerted more pressure with the heel of his boot. He didn't stop until Ryder collapsed in the dirt. "My little sister is stronger than you!" The Morgannai roared.

Ryder hauled himself up to his elbows and knees. "Then she must be a sand buffalo like you," he grumbled. Sand buffaloes were enormous, gluttonous creatures. Ugly, with enormous snouts and slits for eyes, their herds roamed through southern Idonne.

"What did you say?" Thessar growled.

Ryder's temper erupted. All rational thought slipped away. He was sick of Anton's sneering commands, and he didn't care if Thessar pounded him into a heap of flesh. He wasn't going to back down from anyone else today. He stood in front of the giant Morgannai and shouted, "I said she's a sand buffalo like you!"

Thessar's eyes blackened.

Ryder panted, but didn't back away.

"Better than being a desert flea like you. Always hopping around where you're not wanted!" Thessar taunted.

Ryder was shocked to find himself still standing. He'd expected the Morgannai to knock him out with a single club of his meaty fist. "Yes, well even desert fleas serve their purpose."

Thessar's entire body shook with a belly laugh. "Anton's pet is a desert flea."

The epithet scalded Ryder's heart. Is that how the other recruits saw him—as Anton's pet? No wonder they hated him. "It's not like that," he whispered.

"That's exactly what it's like." Thessar's thick finger poked Ryder in the chest with each syllable. When Ryder offered no counter, the Morgannai snorted. He squeezed his finger to his thumb. "And like a flea, you're going to be squashed in the ring!"

Ryder didn't doubt Thessar's prediction, but his pride wouldn't let him quit now. Whatever thrashing awaited him, he would endure it.

When Ryder made no effort to defend himself, Thessar spat in the dirt and lumbered toward the gymnasium.

Their sparring class would begin momentarily. Ryder had no choice but to tag along behind him.

Isolt's Revenge

Ryder stared at the thick stack of parchment on the table. Why was he so hesitant to begin? He rose to stare out the attic's window. The thinnest line of blue on the horizon stirred desires he thought he'd put to rest. He'd thought training with the guard would fulfill him. Initially, the novelty and pleasure of sheer physical exertion had consumed him. But every effort he'd made to befriend other recruits had been rejected. They'd made it clear that he was an outsider, an oddity that didn't belong in their world. Despite his initial optimism that he could make a decent showing in his first fight, with every passing day his confidence flagged. He continued his solo training at night, but at this point, he had to admit that survival would be a positive outcome in his case.

The priesthood embraced him, but the admiration wasn't mutual. No matter what he did, Ryder felt empty. Empty and alone.

The music at the Temple of Delphinus—and these stories about birth and death, and mothers and their children—stirred up questions he'd silenced long ago. Dreams he'd eagerly bargained away returned. Restless dreams of travel, camaraderie, and a purpose that inspired him. A destiny that required every bit of him, not a split of body and mind.

He sighed. No clear answers arrived.

Ryder turned to the table and hunched over the parchment. He forced himself to read the words before him. His imagination brought the words to life as he lost himself in Faerie.

❖ ❖ ❖

It wasn't Flora's usual day to forage for herbs. She'd planned to bake a blueberry pie. Not that she needed it. Short and squareish, with a large, hooked nose that was too harsh for the rest of her wrinkled face, she'd developed the habit of eating treats to ease her isolation.

But a voice said, *"I have something special for you today."*

Flora swiveled her head. Who had spoken?

"It's waiting for you."

She whirled again.

"Go and find what I have left for you at the base of the mountain."

Flora squinted.

"You know which mountain I speak of."

Silence returned.

Flora's eyes settled on Bella, the only other sentient creature in the room. The long-haired black cat lazed on the scrubbed floor of Flora's immaculate cottage, gnawing on a claw. Bella hadn't heard the voice, nor had the voice emanated from the feline. The cat had never spoken.

Puzzled, Flora righted the plaid kerchief she always wore to contain her wild nest of greying hair. The cloth had slipped over her forehead as she'd wheeled from side to side. Her stiff, gnarled fingers toyed with its knot beneath her chin. If she ignored the voice, her days would remain the same, one following another in wearying monotony. Maybe it was time for a change. Maybe it was time for something special.

She set out a bowl of goat's milk for Bella, smoothed her rumpled apron, and waddled out her back door.

Flora arrived at the base of the southernmost peak of the Ruadain by early afternoon. Her sharp gaze roamed across tufted grass to the shadows cast by clumps of trees. She searched the patches of dry dirt beneath her feet, careful to avoid any mud. A misstep in the Balyudor's black muck and she wouldn't be able to swish the caking from her boots with any stream of water. She'd have to sit on her back porch, gouging at the tender leather with a hand knife for three days to get them clean. Her boots might be as old and scuffed as she was, but they were comfortable.

Except for the occasional bird whistle and her own heavy breathing, the surroundings were still. She rested on a large rock and wiped her brow.

A sparkle caught her eye.

Flora heaved herself up, her body shifting from side to side as she forced a casual pace. The edge of the woods wasn't far. It was possible there were eyes watching from the dense undergrowth.

Flora scanned the vicinity once more before she leaned over to touch the thing. The thick skin of her finger pads ran along the silver rim encrusted with sparkling gemstones in every color. There was an indentation in the shallow center of the basin. It was filled with dirt and twigs.

Grey clouds gathered overhead. Flora grimaced. The smell of

the Great White Sea saturated the wind.

She searched the tree line and glade once more and spied them: white bones picked clean. Flora nudged one with the toe of her boot. *Maybe a dwarf or a troll.* She kicked another one. *No, it was too long. A muannaye?* If so, he or she was long deceased. *Maybe the previous owner of something special.* Flora dragged the basin away.

It wasn't heavy, for the craftsmanship was masterful. Only its size made the treasure bulky and unwieldy for someone of Flora's height.

She headed toward the ocean.

The coast was rocky. To the north were cliffs, but to the south was an easy walking path.

Flora followed it to a deserted crescent of beach. She dragged the basin along behind her. If the bowl was responsible for the remains she'd found beside it, that spoke of magic—dwarf magic, most likely. And the metalwork of dwarves was nigh indestructible. So she didn't worry as she pulled her treasure through the sandy grit littered with seed-sized pebbles.

When she came to the water's edge, Flora shifted the basin upright. The bowl mirrored the diffuse light streaming through the breaking clouds above. She grunted as she used her hands to fill the basin with sea water. Swirling it around, she flushed out the grains of debris that had survived her walk. She filled the basin one more time for good measure.

A silvery mist rose from the basin's center.

The voice spoke again, *"You found it. I knew you would."*

Flora whirled around.

Overhead, the grey clouds roiled into a single mass. The sky rumbled. *"Shhhhhh. Isolt sleeps. We must not wake her."*

Flora squinted into the woods. Her gaze traveled the height of the mountain and returned to the ceiling of dark clouds. As soon as she lowered her head, the water in the basin rippled.

"You, above all others, will appreciate what you're about to witness," the voice said.

Flora leaned closer to the water in the bowl.

An image of a young woman with raven hair appeared on the water's surface. The picture enlarged. A man stood near her.

Flora recognized the dull sheen of the mortal world before her large nose grazed the water. She snapped her head back.

Faint voices rose from within the basin.

The young woman stretched her long, slim arm and reached

with desperate, grasping fingers. "Return my wings at once!"

The man's smile mocked her. He clutched a cloak of magnificent white feathers in his hand.

The young woman flinched as he stuffed the faerie wings into a sack like a bundle of rags. "I'm the Faerie Princess Luisa Albiana. You can't take my wings!"

Flora dug the heel of her hand into her breastbone as if just hearing the name *Albiana* caused her physical pain. Her breathing became labored.

"Today is my nineteenth birthday. If I don't return to the Cathedral Palace for my party, my mother, Queen Olivia, will suffer no end of grief." Luisa pointed a finger at the man. "And you'll be to blame!"

Now, Flora took a good look at him. He was tall with yellow hair. No one she recognized. But why would she?

"I've never seen anyone with eyes the color of yours," he said. "Can you spin straw into gold?"

Luisa trembled. "I cannot. My wings!"

"If I keep them, you'll have to become my wife. Isn't that the way it works? Did you say a faerie princess? What about jewels?"

The faerie's face turned a fierce red as she raised the flat of her hand to slap the man's face.

"Oh now, temper, temper." He caught her arm and held it as she struggled. "Come along. What did you say your name was? Luisa? My name is Ben Silver. Don't you have some special power for creating gold coins?" The young man pushed and pulled the faerie princess deeper into the woods.

The image faded away.

"Did you enjoy the show?" the voice asked Flora.

She grunted noncommittally while her thoughts spun in all directions. What recklessness had driven a Daughter of Light across the boundaries of time and space?

"An Albiana in the mortal world presents opportunities for the both of us." The voice arrived at the conclusion Flora's mind groped for. By exposing their potent consciousness to the coarseness of the mortal world, the line of queens had placed themselves at risk. Now Luisa was trapped there.

"Only if it's the beginning of the end of their reign," Flora grumbled.

The voice laughed. The laughter seemed to vibrate through Flora.

She swirled the water in the basin once more. No more images appeared. The show was over. Good thing. It was getting late, and she needed to get home to feed Bella—and herself.

She emptied the silver bowl before balancing it against her back. Once it was centered, she gripped the wide sides with both hands and trudged back through the Balyudor.

SPLAT!

She flew face first to the ground. The silver basin rode up her back and slipped over her head like a helmet. Unable to see or hear anything other than her heart pounding in her chest, she braced herself for blows. None came. Flora stretched her fingers to the basin's rim. She lifted the metal covering enough to peer through a crack.

A sparrow whistled. A distant pitter patter of feet. Probably a troll—female, she guessed—moving away from her. Flora pulled herself to all fours, letting the basin serve as a shield.

The clearing was empty.

She rose to her knees. Twisting her torso from side to side, she grunted when she saw what had tripped her.

A braid of tree roots.

Flora studied the silver basin. It was better than blueberry pie. She returned the unusual gift to her back and hurried home.

Isolt lost herself in the sound of her voice, echoing from the cavern's walls. Her singing was the only thing that soothed her.

The basin's eye had opened a second time. It was unusual magic, to see the one who peered into the bowl, and what that one viewed. It seemed as though Isolt herself was the window. She gazed to the left to watch the faerie princess and mortal man. She looked to the right and saw the square-faced one who resembled a dwarf, yet was different, her hooked nose so close that Isolt tried to touch it. A disheartening effort when only air existed where the water spirit's fingers had once been. Even after all these years, it was difficult to remember her body had dissolved.

Only consciousness remained.

After killing the muannaye, Isolt took greater care when gazing through Ormrun's eye. That first death had been a careless mishap. After being buried alive for eons, the simple sight of clouds and sky framing the muannaye's face had ignited Isolt's rage. A victim herself, she had no desire to kill more innocents.

Perhaps the voice could help her channel the power of the dwarf magic.

It was courting her. Wooing her. It cared for Isolt and her grief, caressing her disembodied essence with the sympathy of an ethereal lover.

Isolt sang into the darkness. Notes of hope touched the melancholy of her song.

If she could kill a muannaye, then she could end a mage's life as well. Isolt pulled Quasimi's face from the anguish of her memories. She held it in her mind.

Flora grew attached to the basin. It filled hours of loneliness.

As mist began to rise from its center, she spoke to her cat. "Needs sea water." An empty pitcher stood on the table between them. There was a well behind Flora's cottage, deep enough to reach a water table fed by the Great White Sea.

When the mist from the basin settled, Flora watched two figures in the woods: Luisa Albiana, who sat on a stone, still wingless, and a young girl, who stood before her. The girl had a bright glow about her and favored Luisa so strongly that she had to be the faerie's daughter. She had no wings either.

"Mommy, what are these?" the young girl held up something large, white and feathery.

"My darling, where did you find them?"

"In a metal box beneath father's bed."

"Gabriela, darling, you discovered the key!" The sound of Luisa's joy reverberated. She embraced the girl.

"But Mommy, what are they?"

Luisa's hand wiped her eyes before she reached for them. "Darling, these are my wings."

"You don't have wings."

"Gabriela, I'm a faerie."

The girl laughed. "You're not a faerie. I am." She spread her arms and twirled. "I'm a faerie princess."

Luisa hugged her wings to her chest.

The girl stopped spinning. "Mommy, why are you crying?"

A river ran behind the rock Luisa sat upon. She patted the space next to her and her daughter joined her. "I must confide in you."

Flora's mind spun. Luisa had given birth to a daughter in the mortal world.

Luisa ran her fingers through her daughter's straw-colored hair. "Gabriela, there are many worlds."

"You mean like planets?"

"No, Gabriela, this mortal world—with its planet and galaxies within its universe—is one world, but there are other worlds."

"Where are they?" the girl asked.

"They are in our hearts, our memories, and our dreams. They also exist on other planes and in other times. Darling, they're all part of the Whole."

"But Mommy, if there are other worlds, how do we visit them? And why don't they talk about them in school?"

"Because your teacher doesn't know they exist."

A puzzled look formed in the girl's large, grey-blue eyes.

"Mommy is from one of those other worlds."

The girl jumped from the rock, turned, and stared at her mother.

"I wasn't born here—on this Earth. My home is elsewhere. I've always wanted to return, but your father ..." the faerie faltered. "Your father held my wings. He knew that as long as he kept them from me, I was tied to the mortal world."

"He doesn't want you to leave!"

Luisa laid the wings down on the stone beside her and embraced the girl. "Maybe he didn't. But I can't stay here another day. If your father takes my wings again, I'll be trapped here forever. I don't think I can survive that. You're the only thing keeping me alive—"

The girl wiggled out of her mother's embrace. "You can't leave!" She began to cry.

"Gabriela, I would take you if I could, but the laws governing the mortal and enchanted worlds won't allow it. A faerie mother is prohibited from taking her child to the enchanted world if their mortal father hasn't broken his faerie troth. And of all the things your father has done to hurt me, that isn't one of them. You must remain with him unless you find a way to come to my world on your own. But I can't be the one to take you there."

Flora absorbed the full impact of what she witnessed: the faerie princess abandoning her first-born daughter in the mortal world. Who would succeed her to the throne?

The girl continued to cry.

Luisa placed a finger firmly beneath her daughter's chin and forced the girl to meet her gaze. "The time has come. I must go now." She kissed her daughter's cheeks.

Flora gasped as Luisa picked up her wings and held them behind her back as though they were a cape. They seamlessly attached to her body, fluttering for a few moments. Then Luisa walked into the middle of the river and disappeared.

Quasimi strolled along the main deck of his ship, the Fair Lady. Tugging at the braid of his greying beard, he listened to the shouts of the crew rise above the sound of the wind. Rufus, his black spider monkey, sat upon his shoulder. Although the sky was clear, the air was cool and damp.

Along the distant horizon Quasimi could just begin to

distinguish the layer of grey that blanketed the northern Realm of Faerie.

The mage approached the ship's railing.

With a new coat of sleek, black paint on her hull to keep her fast, and freshly bleached white sails, the Fair Lady looked every part the beautiful maiden of the sea.

Quasimi loved the schooner almost as much as he loved life itself and was unsettled by a strong sense that this would be their final voyage together. He reached deep into one of the pockets in his brightly colored tunic and withdrew a few shelled pecans. Absentmindedly, he handed them to Rufus, who eagerly snapped them up and popped them into his mouth. "I'm old this morning, Rufus. I feel the chill of the air in my fingers and knees." His aging had hastened since he'd lost the oak wand.

Rufus continued to pat the mage's turban while pointing toward the Realm of Faerie, which was gradually becoming a visible land mass.

"Yes, that's where we're going, Rufus. It's not my favorite place." Quasimi kept his sight on their destination as he spoke. "I wouldn't return if the reason were not so urgent."

Rufus screamed in Quasimi's ear.

"Rufus, that hurt!" The mage covered his ear as the monkey

pounded his turban in growing agitation. "Rufus, please stop!"

The monkey stopped its antics.

"I promise, we'll not stay long enough for any harm to come to us. I'll take care of my business, and we'll leave with haste when I'm done."

Rufus pulled again upon Quasimi's golden earring.

"Yes, it is a woman. However, it's not what you think, you rascal." Quasimi pulled a few more pecans out of his pocket and handed them to Rufus. "They claim she is beautiful and powerful, that she dwells in a magnificent palace that built itself around her, stone by stone. Who could command such acclaim and awe? If Isolt has risen, then Vulcan's rage will be great. I must confirm it isn't her. I must see with my own eyes." Quasimi stroked his beard. "If it's not her, then who?"

It was late in the afternoon when the boatswain laid anchor a few miles from the cove.

Through his spyglass, Quasimi gazed at the twinkling lights of Aldaine and its crowning jewel, the stronghold of Calashai, glittering atop the northernmost peak of the Ruadain as the sun set behind it.

Quasimi faced his crew as he folded the spyglass. "Tonight we'll remain on board the Fair Lady. Tomorrow morning a small group will go ashore."

The next morning, Quasimi, Rufus, and three crewman fought to paddle a small boat across the large waves. The clouds were thick, and the cold winds whipped their hair and clothes. Rugged bluffs lined the massive shoreline. Seagulls circled and screeched overhead as the small crew ground ashore upon the inlet's flat, wet beach.

Two stunning creatures descended the steps carved into an otherwise sheer granite cliff. Male, with dark plaited hair and bronzed skin, their well-fitted coats flared at the waist. As they came closer, Quasimi noted one had eyes of chocolate, while the other's were the color of a clear sky. In all his travels, the mage had never seen creatures as physically perfect as these.

"Welcome to Tyrannis. These steps"—one of the creatures waved his arm above his head—"lead to the home of Elendah, the regent of the stronghold of Calashai. All who come in peace are regarded as friend. My name is Alrick." He took a deep bow. "And this is my brother, Yrrick."

He also bowed low. "We'll escort you to the palace and insure your stay is comfortable." Yrrick smiled and stepped back a courteous distance as Alrick led them to the staircase.

"There are more than a thousand steps," Alrick said.

After they had walked awhile in silence, Quasimi asked, "What kind are your people?"

"Muannaye, though some call us dark faeries."

"And none of you have wings?"

"We differ from the faeries of flower and field. We don't cross the Maeldun Bridge, nor do we travel to the mortal world. Although of all of the creatures in the Realm, we are the most similar to humans."

"Then you dwell solely in Tyrannis?" Quasimi asked.

"Yes," Alrick replied. "You'll find many of our kind in Aldaine, but the largest population lives southeast in the valley cradled by the Undine River."

"I found myself in these lands long ago," the mage mused. "Your kind did not dwell here then."

"We're a novel breed." Alrick turned to look Quasimi up and down. "And you must be very old."

"I am," the mage murmured, "and these steps won't let me forget it for a moment."

Quasimi resisted the urge to sprawl on the thick cushion of grass when they reached the top. Alrick didn't slow his pace. The mage followed the muannai through the palace gates into a huge courtyard. From the sea, the stronghold had sparkled. From the edge of the bluff, it appeared dull, without color. As they drew nearer, its stone walls danced in shades from the lightest amaranth and copper, to sea-washed white. The mage's curiosity increased.

Alrick led Quasimi into the Welcoming Chamber. "Please, rest here. I'll send for refreshments."

Even though his heels, knees, and thighs ached, Quasimi's trepidation kept him on his feet. He paced among the small, well-polished wooden tables, luxurious lounges, and sofas in hues of peach, orange, yellow and gold. A young female muannaye dressed in a flowing golden gown arrived with refreshment. Quasimi couldn't help but stare as she set out steaming pots of tea and vanilla cakes.

Alrick returned to announce, "Elendah will receive you tonight at the evening meal. I'll escort you to your quarters, where you may bathe and dress."

Quasimi followed Alrick through the Grand Entrance Hall to a stone stairway. They climbed a flight of stairs. Alrick unlocked the first door in the corridor. The mage crossed the suite to walk out onto a tiny patio. Below him, the Great White Sea crashed against the wall of mountain. It felt as though he was suspended in midair over the roaring waters. The wind was biting and wet. "Tell me, your lady, is she a muannaye like yourself?"

"She has no wings, but she is no muannaye," Alrick said. He spun on his heels and was gone.

"I'm worried, Rufus." Quasimi retrieved a leather pouch concealed beneath his tunic. He withdrew a folded document. He opened it and flattened it upon the table. It was a map of the Realm of Faerie as it had been in the beginning. The seven mountains of the Ruadain were clearly marked. Quasimi had buried Isolt beneath the northernmost peak. He tugged at his beard. It was the same peak upon which the stronghold sat. "How is it possible she has risen when I buried the key with her?"

Rufus crawled down into Quasimi's lap and wrapped his long, wiry arms around Quasimi's waist. The mage smiled and scratched the monkey behind the ears.

"Whoever the lady of this palace is, she is powerful in the ways of manifestation. I can think of none other than Isolt who might have such strength. Will she recognize me?"

Quasimi entered the bath chamber and stood before the mirror. Where years ago his beard and mustache had been jet black, now they were patched with grey. He removed his turban. Long, grey-streaked hair flowed from his scalp. He found a sharp razor on the vanity and cut the braid from his beard.

When Alrick returned, he gasped in surprise, "I truly would not have known you!"

Quasimi was pleased with the success of his transformation. He rubbed his hand along his clean-shaven chin.

The muannaye led Quasimi into a dining area sealed off by two rosewood screens, inlaid with mirrors. In the center of the space, an elegant table was set for two. "Elendah will be here shortly," was all that Alrick said before he left.

A petite, stout creature wearing a starched white apron over a moss-colored gown slipped through a gap in the screens. She offered Quasimi a glass of dark wine. After he sipped the contents and approved, she curtsied and rushed back between the partitions.

Another muannaye entered the space and curtsied. "I present Elendah, the regent of the stronghold of Calashai."

Quasimi bolted from his chair—and froze.

The regal lady who appeared was not Isolt of the Waters.

He bowed so deep with relief that Rufus had to jump from his shoulder. "I am Quasimi." The monkey grabbed the mage's wrist. "And this is Rufus. We thank you for your hospitality."

Elendah moved toward him with the grace of a large cat. She was lean beneath her watery, grey silk gown. But it was her extraordinary silver hair, twined high upon her head in intricate braids that captured his attention. The plaits were held in place by ornate combs of white gold, encrusted with diamonds and pink pearls. Her grey-blue eyes sparkled beneath wide lids. Her oval face was long, like her nose, which had the slightest dip at the end. And there wasn't a line or wrinkle upon her face.

"We are pleased to welcome visitors. Especially interesting little ones." Elendah crouched easily with her forearms on her knees. Her inquisitive expression won over the diminutive monkey immediately.

Rufus reached out to shake Elendah's long, outstretched fingers while keeping his other hand gripped around his companion's arm.

"Rufus, you're charming. And where did you say you came from?"

"I didn't say, my lady. I travel from the Hidden City."

"The Hidden City? I've never been there."

"Few have." Now that his great fear had proven unfounded, Quasimi felt exhilarated. "The Hidden City gates are not so welcoming as those of the Calashai."

"So I've heard. Are you a sorcerer?"

"I prefer the term *mage*."

"Ah," Elendah said, as the green-dressed creature re-entered the room with another glass of wine for the hostess.

When she disappeared, Quasimi commented, "She's quite unusual and enchanting."

"Fern and Ivy are twins." Elendah moved to one of the chairs. Spreading the folds of her gown evenly around her, she looked up at Quasimi. "They're trolls."

"Trolls?" Quasimi was confused. All the trolls he'd known were ill-shapen, with bulbous noses, oversized ears, sparse heads of hair, clumsy hands and protruding bellies.

"It's little known that the females of the species are quite alluring. They move so quickly that only the sharpest eyes can spot them in the wilds. A few are inclined to make their home with me in the stronghold."

Quasimi moved to sit across the table from her.

Elendah clapped her hands and another little creature came running. She looked exactly like the other, except her gown was a deep plum. Elendah whispered in her ear and she left.

Fern and Ivy quickly returned with bowls of vegetable soup and a platter of fruit and nuts.

"Please, let us start before it cools." Elendah waited for Quasimi to find his spoon and take a sip of the steaming broth.

"It's marvelous," he said.

"We have wonderful cooks in Tyrannis. They're all dwarves. Can you believe it?"

"I didn't know dwarves could cook."

"I'm told that thousands of years ago, the dwarves left the mortal world in haste. They traveled through Tyrannis to the beach you arrived at this morning. A longboat waited in the cove to carry them to Misgradde, all at the hand of a sorcerer."

Quasimi choked on his soup. He covered his mouth with his napkin as heat flushed his face.

"Are you all right?"

Just as Elendah clapped her hands, Quasimi recovered his breath.

Ivy was at Elendah's side.

Quasimi ran his napkin across his forehead. "I'm fine. It's so delicious. I ate too greedily."

"Then you're ready for the next course?"

He nodded as he wet his throat with another sip of wine.

Ivy removed the empty bowls. She returned with a platter of steaming eggplant, squash, and tomato on a bed of crisp greens.

"What was I saying? I can hardly remember," Elendah said.

"You were saying something about an exodus of dwarves."

Quasimi made his tone as nonchalant as possible.

"Ah, yes. A few remained. They're amazing chefs."

"I had no idea." Quasimi had recovered his composure.

"And what brings you to our country?" Elendah asked.

"I heard tales about a new breed of creature, so I came to explore," Quasi extemporized.

"You speak of the muannai, the dark faeries?"

Fern and Ivy cleared the table and brought a steaming pumpkin and potato tart.

"And what kind are you? For you are no muannaye," Quasimi observed.

"No, I'm not. But like them, I have no wings and am unable to pass to the mortal world."

Quasimi pondered upon the puzzle of her identity. "Your skin is pale and your hair—such an extravagant silver."

Elendah turned her head.

Quasimi watched her closely. He'd seen her kind before. It had been ages ago. "Why, you're a grey faerie!" The mage pointed at her with his fork. "The Isle of Minnanon. That is where I've seen your kind before."

"You've visited the island?"

"I have. It's far north of here. The population of grey faeries dwindles. There can't be more than fifty alive. How did you end up here?"

"I was a foundling. A seagull carried me to these lands. An elderly woman cared for me. However, when I turned nineteen, she vanished. I traveled the coast and woods for years alone. The first time I made the journey up this mountain, I fell in love with its proximity to the Great White Sea. When I came back the second time, the stronghold of Calashai awaited me. I confess it's quite the mystery who actually built my home."

The mage put down his fork and gazed deeply into Elendah's eyes. "The force of your desire is powerful."

"You think I built this?" She indicated the walls around them with her pale hands. "With my desire?"

Quasimi shook his finger at her. "I believe that you built this castle with the strength of your desire alone."

"The stronghold has always felt like more than a home," she mused.

"Like a second skin, perhaps?"

Elendah blushed. "A mage from the Hidden City, you must know a few tricks."

"I create illusions."

"And how do you do that?" she asked.

"I reach into the person before me and pull out their longing. From that I am able to create whatever they most wish to see."

"To deceive and manipulate."

"I cannot stray from what is dear to their heart."

"Would you create an illusion for me?"

Quasimi carefully wiped his mouth with his napkin. "I think not." He had no desire to reach into such a powerful faerie so close to the place of Isolt's enchantment. When she didn't press, he relaxed.

"Will you be staying long in Faerie?" she asked.

"No."

"If your magic is illusions, you must visit the Veiled Tavern. Those who spend a night in the inn are shown their own greatest illusion, if they sleep well."

"Has my lady had such an experience?" Quasimi asked respectfully.

Elendah swirled her wine. "I have not. But for one who deals in such things, it would make a worthwhile trip."

"You make a valid point. But my crew is not prepared to travel on land."

"They're welcome to stay here. I could provide you a horse and supplies. You seek adventure. You can travel there and back in less than a moon cycle. I think you must go."

Quasimi pulled absentmindedly on his beardless chin. "Would you accompany me?"

"I must decline."

"Making the trip without the pleasure of your company is not quite as enticing."

"I know the proprietor, Gumf. Mention that you come by way of the stronghold. He'll make sure your needs are well attended to."

"You so want me to go."

Elendah's eyes sparkled. "I do."

"If I go, will you travel with me to the Isle of Minnanon upon my return?"

Elendah laughed. "Why do I feel like you'll not accept no for an answer?"

Quasimi leaned across the table. "Because I won't. The longing in your heart for your own kind is deep, and I would be most honored to escort you to the land of your people. My boat, the Fair Lady, is not luxurious, but she's comfortable and safe. The crew is seasoned, and I would welcome your companionship and conversation."

"Now it is you who makes it difficult for me to say no."

"Then say yes."

"Your trip to the Veiled Tavern will give me time to prepare for a sea voyage. Of what length?"

Quasimi's victory thrilled him. "Several moon cycles. It's farther than the tavern."

Elendah smiled. "It has been a long time since I've traveled beyond Aldaine." She placed her napkin firmly on the table, as if to emphasize her decision. "Alrick will prepare a horse and supplies for your trip to the tavern. They'll be ready for you in the morning."

Quasimi rose from the table. "It has been my great pleasure."

Elendah nodded gracefully. When Rufus settled on Quasimi's shoulder, she gave the monkey a final rub behind his ears.

The mage couldn't refrain from making one more request. "While I'm gone, I wonder if you might find one of those dwarves who cook so well, one who might be interested in traveling the seas. I have a cook, but he would much prefer to be a sailor. I would pay him well."

"I'll see what I can do."

"Thank you, Elendah, regent of the stronghold of Calashai. I'd be most indebted." Quasimi bowed deeply. "Now Rufus and I must get some sleep. Apparently, we face a new adventure in the morning."

✧ ✧ ✧

The horse the stable provided for the trip was strong and healthy. There was a well-made saddle and the two side-packs bulged with supplies.

Rufus settled upon Quasimi's shoulder and the pair departed. The mage had left his turban and tunics in his room. He traveled in the style of the muannaye, wearing knee-high boots and fitted pants.

After passing through the stronghold's front gates, they followed the main road as it spiraled through the city of Aldaine. If Quasimi had not been in such a hurry to return to the stronghold, he might have dallied in the city. The tearooms in particular appealed to his penchant for news and conversation. Another time. He wished to return to Elendah as soon as possible.

After a few hours, the stone road gave way to a dirt one. They were well beyond the densely-populated crown of the mountain now.

Quasimi spotted an undersized bearded creature wearing an enormous red cone hat in the distance. Pointing it out to Rufus, he said, "That is a gnome. They're antisocial and grumpy."

Just before dusk they came to the base of the mountain and set up camp.

On the morning of the ninth day, Quasimi reached the Balyudor. He withdrew the map and a metal compass from the leather pouch that hung beneath his shirt. After studying the map, he bade the horse enter the woods. They were dense and tangled with enormous tree trunks and much undergrowth. Even the grey clouds overhead had been swallowed by a tangle of limbs and vines.

It wasn't long before they heard a gravelly sing-song voice:

Finders keepers, losers cry

Silver saucer caught my eye,

Shining stones sparkling bright

Now it's mine, bones lie close by.

Intrigued, the mage tracked the sound of the rhyming song. Rufus pushed vines away as they made their way through the woods. There was space for the horse to walk, but no real trail.

The rhyming continued:

Finders keepers, losers cry

Silver saucer caught my eye,

Shining stones sparkling bright,

Now it's mine, bones lie close by.

Without warning, the impenetrable undergrowth gave way to a

picturesque white picket fence surrounding a well-maintained yard. Light breaking through the clouds illuminated a wooden A-frame cottage painted yellow and green. In its windows, flower boxes burst with drapes of heavy lilac-colored blooms, and smoke curled from the chimney. Chickens ran loose around a goat tied to a post. A gate marked a little stone walkway that meandered to the front door.

No wind rustled the leaves of the twisted ficus trees, and the sparrows had fallen quiet.

The mage traveled around the outside perimeter of the fence.

In the backyard, a stout little woman stood upon a platform, vigorously stirring the contents of a large wooden barrel. Half his height, she wore a long, red-patterned dress. A patterned kerchief covered her head. She hadn't spied Quasimi yet, and continued to sing as she stirred the thick liquid frothing inside the tub.

Finders keepers, losers cry,

Silver saucer caught my eye,

Shining stones sparkling bright,

Now it's mine, bones lie close by.

"Good morning," the mage shouted.

The lady froze. Although she stopped singing, she maintained the grip upon her mixing stick. She surveyed the clearing. As soon as she saw Quasimi, she threw the stick against the side of the barrel and dropped her hands to wipe them on her apron. She walked over to the mage, her square body tilting from side to side on her short legs.

"Well, it might be a good morning, but then again, it might not be." Both her voice and demeanor were gruff. "I suppose that would depend on who you are and what you want." The little old woman planted her short, stout girth opposite Quasimi and his horse with her hands on her hips. Although the fence stood between them, her head moved without pause as she looked him up and down, taking his measure.

When her brown irises flickered with recognition, Quasimi's curiosity deepened. He was certain he'd never seen her before.

"My name is Quasimi, and this is my friend, Rufus. We're traveling to the Veiled Tavern by way of Aldaine, as friends of Elendah, the regent of the stronghold of Calashai. Your clever rhyming intrigued us."

The lady waved her hand. "Flattery is the deceit of the cunning and well-connected."

Determined not to be put off by her brusque demeanor, Quasimi dismounted.

165

Rufus alighted from his shoulder to balance in the saddle.

Keeping hold of the horse's reins, the mage performed a ceremonious bow. "We don't wish to interfere with your work. Your rhyming is impressive, your home is charming. We bid you good day, madam, and regret there's not time to deepen our acquaintance."

Her fists, thrust into her apron pocket, twitched. "I'm almost done making my soap." She took three steps closer to the fence, wrapped her hands around the top posts, and rose up on her tiptoes to peer over it. "We don't get many visitors in these parts." Her scrutiny of Rufus intensified. "Actually, we don't get any. My name is Flora. I've baked a fresh apple tart which should be cooled by now. Why don't you"—she stared openly at the spider monkey—"and that little black devil join Bella and me for a bite."

"Bella?"

Flora indicated the black cat elongated on her back porch.

"Apple tart, you said?"

Flora headed back toward the cottage, her short, stumpy body swaying from side to side. "Warm, fresh baked. Come around to the front gate. Clover, my goat, will enjoy your horse's company."

She was halfway across the yard. Quasimi led the horse around the fence as she directed.

By the time he entered the gate, and tied up the horse next to the goat, Flora had opened the front door of her little home and was waving them in.

Rufus executed a graceful leap from the saddle to land on Quasimi's shoulder.

"I'd like that little devil to sit on my shoulder just like that," Flora said as Quasimi dipped his head to fit through her front door.

The smell of freshly cooked apples and cinnamon filled the air. A small table with four chairs stood to the side. A kettle hung over a fireplace in the center of the back wall. Bella sat before it, a statue high upon her front paws. Like Flora, the cat was focused on Rufus.

Flora pulled back a chair from the table and motioned with her hand to Quasimi. "Sit, sit."

He awkwardly folded himself into the undersized chair.

Rufus stood upon the table and made faces at the unimpressed Bella.

Flora served herself and Quasimi generous quarters of pie. "You'll like it." Before she sat down, she gazed at Rufus, still trying to make an impression on Bella. "You'll have to make more of a fuss to get a rise out of my cat. Will he eat apple tart?" she asked Quasimi.

"I don't know."

She returned to the counter and placed a third quarter of tart on a plate. "This is the best treat you'll ever taste. Bella won't touch it. But I always say she doesn't know what she's missing." Flora slid the pie toward the monkey and sat down to partake of her own piece.

Rufus poked the crust with his fingers and licked them.

"He likes it," Quasimi said.

Flora stared unabashedly at the mage. "What business do you have at the Veiled Tavern?"

"Elendah sent me. She believes the curious nature of the tavern might hold some interest for me."

"I've heard quite a bit about the regent, although I've yet to meet her myself. What is she like?"

"Beautiful, gracious. She's a grey faerie."

Flora wiped her hand with her mouth. "Didn't know there were any grey faeries in these parts. Where are you from?"

Her bluntness amused Quasimi. "The Hidden City."

"I've read about that place." Flora pointed to one of the bookshelves. "One of those books has a story in it about a mage from there, *Isolt's Enchantment.*"

Quasimi remained impassive. It wasn't surprising the tale had been recorded, only that the stout little creature had no inkling it was about him.

"Are you a mage?"

"Indeed, I am."

"Huh. Would you like some hot tea? I've got a stew simmering in the kettle. You could stay for lunch. Where did you get that little devil?"

"He was a gift."

"From who?"

"A mortal who was grateful for services rendered."

"Humph," was Flora's response, as she waddled over to the fireplace.

Finders keepers, losers cry,

Silver saucer caught my eye—

"That was the rhyme you were singing when we arrived," Quasimi interrupted. "What does it mean? You've been singing it over and over."

"Just a funny little rhyme running through my head," Flora's eyes darted from side to side as she took tea leaves from a container and placed them into two cups.

Her craftiness baited Quasimi. He rallied his powers and reached deep within her. A monumental loss saddened her. It had left her damaged and withdrawn. Flora craved the feeling of kinship with fellow spirits.

No physical alteration would be required for Quasimi to manifest an illusion that would satisfy her heart's desire. A simple façade of sincere caring was all that was needed. "Flora, you're right, this apple tart is simply the best I've ever tasted. It was so kind of you to invite us to share it with you, and a cup of tea sounds delightful."

When her back was to him, he extended his hands and stretched his fingers to concentrate his power of mesmerism. She would now respond to him as if he were the close companion she craved.

When Flora returned to the table with two teacups, she appeared more at ease. "Does the little devil drink tea?"

"Probably not."

Flora sat down in her chair and pulled the bowl of honey toward her. After taking a huge quantity for her tea, she pushed the bowl toward Quasimi.

"I have a secret," Flora said as the mage added a few drops of honey into his cup.

"Well, you mustn't tell me what it is," said Quasimi.

"It's hard to keep a secret from a good friend."

"I imagine it must be."

"We could be good friends, you and I."

"We could, Flora. We could be very good friends."

"I go to the Veiled Tavern once a week. They buy my soap with coins that I keep hidden."

"Is that your secret, Flora?"

Her eyes narrowed. "I have a much bigger secret than that. I could show you. You won't tell anyone, will you?"

Quasimi ran his fingers across his lips as if to seal them tight.

Flora became more animated. "One day, I went out searching for flowers and herbs. I use them to scent my soaps. I was over by the Ruadain, farther than I normally go, when a sparkle caught my eye. There's never any sunshine out there, but it caught the light of the grey skies just the same. That's how shiny my secret is."

Quasimi shifted in his chair.

Flora's eyes shined. "When I tiptoed closer to the sparkle, I saw the bones. They were picked clean. Whoever they belonged to had been dead a long while."

The mage sat still as a stone. A chill gathered at the base of his spine. "But what sparkled, Flora? What drew your attention in the

171

first place?"

"It was a silver saucer with pretty colored stones decorating its rim. But it was the bones that alerted me: The bowl's value is greater than its beauty."

A sense of doom slithered across the back of Quasimi's neck. Thinking it might be an insect, he tried to brush it away. "The bones?"

She was so involved in her tale, Flora didn't seem to register his discomfort. "Bones on the ground, fancy metalwork close by, death in the air." She widened her hands in a display of wonder. "I couldn't believe it. I said to myself, 'You've stumbled upon some dwarf relic infused with magic'."

Quasimi's impulse to leap from the cramped chair wasn't due to physical discomfort.

"Do you want to see it?" she asked.

"You have it here, in your home?"

Her smile finally reached her eyes. "That's my secret." She rose and disappeared through the single interior door.

Quasimi ran his palm across his damp forehead. He undid the top buttons of his shirt. Used to his free-flowing garments, the fitted clothes stifled him. Why had he strayed from his course? What had compelled him to toy with Flora? Whatever it was, it had been a foolish impulse. He needed to withdraw his illusion of kinship and flee.

She returned with a bulky item covered in cloth. She dragged it across the floor and settled it in the middle of the cottage. She retrieved a pitcher from the cupboard. She had to carry it with both hands. "The well in my backyard reaches a water table fed by the Great White Sea. It's the only water that will awaken the saucer's magic."

"Really?" Quasimi's voice quavered.

Flora set the pitcher down and carefully unwrapped the package. "It's like an eye."

A silver basin shined in the cottage's dim light, beguiling the mage. He rose from the small table to inch toward it. "Flora, it's magnificent. Someone would pay you a pretty piece for this."

"Someone like you?" she wheedled.

Quasimi couldn't take his gaze from the basin. "You would only have to name your price."

She picked up the pitcher. "I don't want to sell it."

He winced. The desire to possess it consumed him.

"When you fill the basin with water from the Great White Sea, you can see things."

"What can you see?" he asked.

A troubled expression flitted across Flora's wrinkled face. She filled the basin. "Look for yourself."

The mage kneeled on the floor to be closer to the riveting object.

Flora placed a hand on his back and encouraged him. "Go ahead, look. I want to know what it shows you."

The basin compelled his gaze.

Quasimi reached forward to grip the gem-encrusted rim with one hand and then the other. He balanced on his toes before rising to his full height in the center of the room. Once he leveled the water, a cloud-colored mist rose from the water's placid surface. His fingers clutched tighter and tighter.

When Isolt's face formed in the water, her eyes black as coal, the mage tried to release the bowl. But it held him. He couldn't let go.

The water in the basin boiled and hissed. The vapor spewing from it darkened to smoke.

Quasimi's air passageways suffocated, but still couldn't free himself from the basin's grip. Its heat seared the skin from his hands.

Flora backed away as Rufus shrieked and covered his ears.

Isolt's vengeance roared through Flora's cottage, igniting

Quasimi into a statue of flames.

As the ancient water elemental raged, the mage's screams—and the sickening smell of his burning flesh—flooded the room.

When Isolt was done with Quasimi, all that remained was a pile of bleached bones in the middle of Flora's home.

As the silver basin clattered to the floor with a great sturm und drang, Rufus jumped from the table and skittered along the floor, waving his spindly arms and legs. The monkey picked up one of the bones, smelled it, and threw it across the room. He put his hands over his ears and began to shriek again.

"There, there." Flora did her best to calm him. "We'll find a nice place for your friend. But me and Bella"—she gazed over at the cat spread out on the floor—"we're glad you're here. Aren't we, Bella?"

The cat curled its neck away from Rufus.

For the first time since she'd found the silver basin, Flora was loathe to touch it. She left it uncovered in the middle of the floor, giving it wide berth as she maneuvered around it. Rarely had Isolt of the Waters shown her face to the spring faerie, and it was now, in the aftermath of Quasimi's death, that Flora put all the pieces together.

Witnessing the flames of Isolt's vengeance had ripped open Flora's own deep wounds and melancholy enveloped her.

Later that evening when Flora garnered the strength to gather Quasimi's bones, Rufus followed her as she waddled to the well in the far corner of her backyard.

"Off to the Great White Sea with you," she said.

Rufus chattered frantically as she dropped the bones down into the frothing well one by one.

"Don't be alarmed," she told the monkey. "There's a rip current in the well that will carry his bones out to sea, and you must agree, those mystical waters are a more honorable resting place for his remains than beneath a pile of dirt."

Rufus coiled and uncoiled the creaky chain as if he might draw his friend whole and alive from the well's depths if he persisted.

"There, there, my love." Flora patted the monkey's bowed head. "There's nothing to be done. The lady in the silver bowl was angry with your friend. She's the one who called him here. It wasn't my doing."

The monkey didn't budge.

Flora reached into her apron pocket and brought out a shelled walnut. Rufus snatched it from her hand and tossed into his mouth.

"You like walnuts, my pretty? I've got plenty of those." She went to get the bag she kept in the cupboard. Grabbing a nutcracker, she carried the bag out to the back porch. There she sat with Bella and cracked the shells one after another. Soon she began to sing-song another rhyme:

Got a secret I won't tell,

Unless you pay me very well,

Silver saucer cast a spell,

Bones are buried in my well.

Ryder felt little sympathy for the mage who'd imprisoned Isolt, and effectively murdered her son, simply because Vulcan had instructed him to. But the existence of this Flora, who at one time had possessed Koldis' counterpart Ormrun, puzzled him.

He tried to place her in his mind, but couldn't recall having heard her name before.

Did she still have the basin?

Was it still in Faerie?

"Thessar! Ryder!"

The young priest froze as adrenaline swamped his body. The

head of every recruit in the sparring gymnasium swiveled, searching for the last two first-round combatants.

The intimidating Morgannai sliced through the crowd.

Ryder shook his head. He was going to die. And it was going to hurt. His vision telescoped upon his opponent.

Thessar's huge teeth grinned. His bulky muscled mass strained as he climbed into the ring.

Ryder hadn't taken a single step. He searched the faces in the crowd. Many turned away in dismissal, the rest sneered in contempt. He wouldn't lose their respect if he backed down because they thought so little of him in the first place. The realization shamed him. He forced himself to move. When he reached the ring, the volume of shouts and jeers drowned every thought from his mind.

Ryder groped his way through the rope barriers, his heart bucking like a wild desert horse. The ring-minder, a scrawny Typhon with bruised circles around his eyes, directed Ryder to the corner opposite the hulking Thessar.

When Ryder pivoted to face his opponent, Thessar slammed his fist into his palm.

Ryder's mind blanked. Everything he'd practiced during his nighttime training sessions fell away. Why had he bothered? What idiocy had made him think he could hold his own among these brutal warriors?

As soon as the ring-minder's hand dropped, Thessar rushed Ryder like a crazed bull.

An instinct for survival took over Ryder's body. He lurched sideways. The move was more graceful and decisive than he'd expected, and Thessar tangled in the ropes. Ryder heard cheers. He tried to think as Thessar freed himself.

The Morgannai wasn't grinning when he turned around. His wide nostrils brayed.

Ryder half curled his left hand. He made a fist with his right.

Thessar blocked the punch before Ryder could fully cock his arm. The Morgannai slammed Ryder's jawbone with such force that he swirled and stumbled.

But he didn't topple to the floor although if felt like his teeth cracking together had splintered his face. The shattering pain shocked him to another level of awareness. He crouched and shuffled sideways.

In the ring, no strike was illegal or forbidden. These were street fighters with no code of honorable or dishonorable blows. Their only goal was to best their opponent.

Ryder glared at Thessar's crotch. The Morgannai rushed him

with both fists forming a single club. He raised his arms high to smash the double-fist down on Ryder's skull. Ryder threw his body forward. Thessar battered his right shoulder. Ryder crumpled to his right hip. He managed to roll away before Thessar's right heel could crush down and finish him. He crawled a short distance before he rolled again, onto his back. Thessar shadowed him. Ryder folded his knees into his chest. Thessar retreated.

With his pre-vision, the Morgannai had seen Ryder's plan to slam his heels into the most vulnerable part of his body.

Ryder gulped. How could he hope to survive if Thessar could predict his every move before he made it? Experiencing the reality of the Morgannai's pre-vision was totally different than having it explained by Bardo.

How hard would Thessar beat him if Ryder remained on the ground, unresisting?

The Morgannai zigzagged a few paces away, then he broke into a run. Had he read Ryder's resignation?

Ryder's body took over when Thessar's feet left the ground. The priest swung his left leg in a wide arc. It caught Thessar's bulk and skewed the landing of his belly flop. Ryder rolled again. Before he'd traveled a hand's length, Thessar's elbow crushed into Ryder's back.

Ryder bellowed as Thessar repeated the blow with his other elbow.

Ryder collapsed.

The ring-minder called the match for Thessar.

Although Ryder registered that he was still alive, he made no effort to rise. He couldn't. His body felt like a bag of disjointed, throbbing parts. The ring-minder called for a stretcher. Ryder didn't resist as they lifted him onto the taut canvas. Someone patted his shoulder. "You lasted longer than any of us thought you would."

The entire bout had lasted mere minutes.

The next morning, Ryder pissed blood. He sat on the edge of his stiff cot. Every move he made caused some new part of his body to protest. The guard physician had bandaged his ribs and given him a sticky roll of herb paste to chew on for the pain. The roll was already gone. He couldn't face the sunrise training drills. His obsession with becoming a member of the guard was over.

It was as wrong a fit for him as the Order.

Umbra

Ryder waited anxiously for Garrick and Shilda. In the face of the worst sandstorm that Idonne had seen in years, everyone else had abandoned the visitor's courtyard. Not a leaf rustled where Ryder stood. However, enormous clouds crossed the desert with staggering speed, painting the eastern horizon a red wall of sand. Ryder scanned the road winding from the valley below.

This morning, his chief concern had been how to hide his injuries from the couple who were like a mother and father to him. But now, he worried for their safety. If the familiar cart didn't arrive soon, the storm would engulf them. Although sand twisters were common in Idonne, sandstorms of this magnitude were rare. In his eighteen years, Ryder had seen only one.

"You there! We're locking the gates!"

Ryder waved his hand without turning. The sand could eat him; he wasn't leaving the courtyard until he knew Garrick and Shilda were safe.

A heavy hand slammed down on Ryder's shoulder. "It's not safe out here! You need to get inside the citadel walls."

Ryder spun and looked into Thessar's black eyes. He hadn't seen the Morgannai since the night they'd fought.

"You!" Thessar shouted. "I should have known. Are you mad? What are you doing out here? The storm is pulverizing everything in its path. Not to mention the radlers flying through the air!" Radler snakes burrowed in the plains. A storm like this cracked open their nests and flung them far and wide. Their venom was deadly.

Ryder shrugged the Morgannai's heavy hand from his shoulder. "My friends are out there! I can't go inside until I know they're safe."

Thessar's eyes rounded in disbelief. "I'll say one thing for you, you're fearless."

The unexpected compliment rippled through Ryder. He widened his stance, stood taller, and crossed his arms across his chest with determination. "If you have to lock the gates, then lock me outside."

"Fearless or stupid. They're often the same." The Morgannai stuck his thumb and forefinger in his mouth and whistled. Minutes later two Idonnai Guard, mounted on midnight horses, appeared. "Go with them!" Thessar shouted.

Ryder's jaw dropped. He turned a questioning gaze to the beast who had pummeled him only days before. "Why are you helping me?"

"We're the Idonnai Guard. You're a priest. Our job is to serve and protect you. And those you care for." The Morgannai bowed and stalked away.

One of the guard members held out his hand. "Ride with me. We'll find your friends."

Ryder swung himself into the wide saddle, wincing as pain rippled through his body. He described the baker's cart and mule to the guards. The horses wheeled and barreled down the road, into the valley and straight for the storm.

Fear stretched the eyes and flattened the mouths of the few travelers they passed. Garrick and Shilda weren't among them. The riders raced to meet the wall of sand. They halted a short distance before the approaching maelstrom. The horses danced and snorted. Both guardsmen wrestled to keep them from spinning and bolting.

Ryder dug his knees into his horse's flank to keep from being thrown.

"Once we enter the storm, it will be almost impossible to see!"

"Are you sure they're in there?"

"Yes!" Cool air from Huros collided with dry wind from Idonne, creating gusts that funneled through a gap in the mountains that bordered both countries. Garrick and Shilda would have set out for the citadel early in the morning. By the time they realized the storm chased them, it would have been too dangerous to turn back.

The guardsmen wrapped their heads in sheer scarves. They kicked their horses and the terrified creatures leapt toward the gritty tempest.

"Garrick! Shilda!" Although he could barely hear himself above the roar of the wind, Ryder shouted their names again and again. As they pressed forward, the horses were no longer running. The sheer force of the wind challenged their every step. The dust thickened. Visibility diminished. There was no sign of life.

The guard riding next to them screamed and ducked.

Something wet slapped against Ryder's forehead and slithered away.

"Radlers!" The guard Ryder rode behind fell forward over his horse's neck. "We have to go back!"

Ryder couldn't. "Leave me here!"

"We can't do that!"

"There's a ridge!" Ryder pointed. "Can you wait for me there?" When he slid to the ground, the wind knocked him to his knees. Brutal gusts pushed him down again and again. Red sand infiltrated every crevice and pore in his clothes and his body. He staggered forward, practically blind. He tried to call for Garrick, but choked on a clot of sand. He tripped and slammed his jaw against a hard edge. The sharp pain echoed through his body, awakening every throb and ache his adrenaline-fueled search had numbed. Jagged nausea rose and fell in waves as he waited for the physical agony to subside.

He braced himself for movement and raised his hand. He traced the shape of the surface he sagged against. A long wooden panel. The side of an overturned cart. His flagging energy renewed. He pulled himself along its outline. Around the final corner, Garrick and Shilda huddled with their mule. Ryder fell on top them.

They clutched at him. "The cart overturned!" Garrick shouted. "Shilda's leg is broken!"

"Two Idonnai Guard are not far. I'll go get them. They'll take you and Shilda to the citadel!"

Ryder left them there before they could argue with him. He bent almost in half to keep his eyes on the road swept with sand. He shuffled his feet so he wouldn't veer from the paving. The strength of the wind persisted. The world was an orange-red blur. Everything was grit and roaring, burning and ripping, as he rammed his way through the storm.

He felt his way to the ridge. "I found them! Follow me!"

The guardsmen trudged behind him, leading the terrified horses by their reins. The battle with the wind and the sand never abated. When they reached the cart, the guardsmen mounted their horses. Garrick had created a make-shift splint for Shilda's leg. Ryder lifted her, and with Garrick's help, they settled her behind one of the guardsmen. She moaned, but was able to cling to the rider. Garrick hoisted himself up behind the second guard.

Ryder waved them off. He crawled into the space beneath the broken cart and collapsed.

"Desert Flea!"

He was dreaming.

"Ryder!"

He was awake. He scrambled to see who was calling his name and bumped his head. He groaned, clutching his skull in his hand.

Would the agony never end? A horse rounded the cart. Ryder couldn't believe what he saw. Thessar had come for him.

"We can't leave their mule!" Ryder shouted.

Thessar dismounted. He lifted a coil of rope from his saddle to create a loose halter to loop around the animal's neck.

"I'll ride him!" Ryder yelled.

When they arrived at the barrack's infirmary, Ryder demanded to see Garrick and Shilda. An exception had been made to the exclusion of females in the citadel; Shilda's leg needed to be treated.

Garrick sat by his wife's bed, holding her hand. "It was hard for her to be the patient, but they've taken good care of her," he said. "Thank you for saving us."

Ryder wanted to stay with them, but Thessar called the physician who led Ryder away.

"We'll see you in class when all that"–Thessar pointed to Ryder's head, shoulder, chest, and thigh–"is healed."

As the doctor examined him, Ryder savored the sensation that Thessar's invitation to return to training had produced. The light, airy feeling was as unexpected as the recruit's efforts to help him save Garrick and Shilda. It forced Ryder to reconsider.

Why shouldn't he continue his training? He hadn't been the

only recruit to lose in the sparring ring.

The Guard perceived winning and losing in a much different way than Ryder did. Perhaps it was because they actually faced risk with their bodies and didn't just read about it in books. Thessar and the two guards who had ridden into the sandstorm had refused to abandon Ryder. Their actions were devoted and noble.

The young priest began to wrap his head around the idea that training with the Guard might strengthen his mind and his character as much as his body.

Several days later, Ryder arrived in the attic studio to find Anton there.

Warily, Ryder eased himself onto the bench. The physician had ordered him to return to the infirmary at least once a day until the tenderness and swelling of his various injuries subsided; and Shilda had given him some poultices to speed his healing. Soon, Ryder would be able to return to his classes with the Guard.

Anton said nothing about his training. He indicated the scroll on the table. "Now begins your study of the entity forming in the Void in earnest. As you proceed, I want you to hold this question in your mind: Should the Order support its incarnation?"

"Have you received information about the location of the

basin?" Ryder's mouth was dry. "Is that why you have me studying these things?"

"It will surface, and when it does, I wish the Order to be prepared."

"Then it is no longer in Faerie?"

"It seems unlikely."

"But there have been no reports of its sale ... or theft?"

"There has been no new information or sightings, but I have refrained from direct inquiry. I fear it would arouse the interest of unsuitable parties. The fewer who know of the existence of these artifacts, and their power, the better."

The tension in Ryder's shoulders unlocked. As a newly ordained priest, he had no contact with those beyond the citadel walls who supplied the Order with its vast reservoir of information. It would be several years before he would be invited to cultivate those kinds of relationships. However, knowing that Anton's knowledge of Ormrun had reached a dead end was welcome news.

He waited until the elder priest left him before he began reading.

Dying. Death. Light snuffed out, but not completely. A grey

sheen, its source not visible, infiltrates the vast space I float in. My awareness simmers. I wait. Minutes. Hours. Days. Weeks. Months. Eternity?

A tunnel of warm sticky heat envelops me. Pulls and sucks me deep into its vortex. The timeless nothingness stretches me; thinner, thinner, thinner.

My psyche travels through some cosmic sieve, and I lose ... what is it that I have lost? The brighter part of myself—an ember—falls away. It is gone.

Images from my life, memories—the ones I buried—jangle through me. I'm reminded in vivid detail of every evil I ever committed—from the smallest lie to the most deplorable betrayal. The excuses I made for myself—every rationalization—consolidates into a single trail of gluey telltale.

The sticky thread spins and rolls into a compacted ball of cowardice, envy, self doubt, and self pity. The grey light is extinguished. I have arrived in a void of omnipotent blackness as an impotent, seething blotch.

Heat builds around me, my consciousness implodes. Raining down through the ethers, I am mortal ash.

In the Void, a unifying mass absorbs what were once discrete particles.

✧ ✧ ✧

It's true I fell in love with Isolt of the Waters. But for me, this didn't happen in her youth when she graciously bubbled and flowed upon Una's fecund belly. I didn't even exist then. But I can assure you, if I had, she wouldn't have caught my eye in those days. It's a matter of taste. Personally, I find the untested, the unwounded, the undamaged, dull.

Bring me the scourged, the broken, the failed in their existence. Bring me their remnants, the bones and enduring fragments of their passionate desires. Fired in the flames, I only want what has hardened and set. I don't trust or have faith in anything else.

I am Umbra, the darkest part of the shadow. Born of mortal ash, I dwell in the Void, incorporeal. It is here I discovered Isolt— abandoned, broken-hearted, flooded with grief for her unborn child. I watched from afar as the desire for revenge fed her. Darkened her. Filled her. Recreated her. I thrilled to watch her transform.

My Shadow Queen.

I fell deeply in love. How could I not?

She was parched with a thirst for justice. She refused to forgive the ones who wronged and forgot her.

I completely admired her. Swooned for her. Her essence fortified me as my own strength swirled and gathered in the aphotic depths of the Great White Sea.

I could have loved my queen for eternity.

Honestly, disembodied as we both are, what more was there to hope for?

What a boon when the dwarves created that silver basin.

The magical eye.

I harbored no personal ill will toward Quasimi. I understand there was a time, long ago, when he was the most powerful mage in the Hidden City. However, that was before he lost Hermes' Wand. From that moment on, his powers waned, and he became aged and weak.

When he looked into the basin, I saw the lines spidering from his eyes, the grey of his unshaved face, and the weariness of his soul.

Only an old man remained. The infamous sorcerer was gone.

I didn't expect what happened next. Isolt rose quickly to seize him. With her will, she held him. I saw his thumbs sealed to the rim. He couldn't release the basin.

I'm certain Isolt showed him her face as she shrieked and screamed her angry accusations.

And justly so. It was, after all, Quasimi who cast the spell that bound Isolt—loveless, childless, and now bodiless—beneath the Ruadain.

What did he expect? That she would sleep docilely until the end of time?

No. I do not fault her for what she did next. Truth be told, it was clever. I had expected, up to that moment, for Quasimi to find the same fate as the muannaye, the basin's unfortunate buyer: a whirlwind of anger marching in an army of flames.

But with the one who had banished her into the Void, Isolt was more insidious. She brought him down, into her element. Water. And there she toyed with him.

I witnessed confusion, then anger, and finally horror mask his face as Isolt pulled him to her. Then let him go.

Endlessly, against his will, his head was pulled into the shallow waters of the basin, but for him they became like the drowning waters of the deepest sea. Isolt held him without mercy as he gagged and gasped, swallowing sea water and gulping for air. Just as the peace of unconsciousness loomed, she would release him for a single breath.

But he couldn't release the basin as his face was dragged back into the sea water again and again.

Isolt kept at this for hours.

What Flora and that poor monkey witnessed I will never know. Perhaps they were spared ... a moment on their plane passing as eternity in ours. Yet I, even with my avenging nature, finally turned away. But I could not escape the sharp painful waves of Isolt's shrieks and screams.

Did Quasimi hear her unleash eons of fury?

I'll never know, but I did.

We all did, those of us who call the salt waters of the Great White Sea and the nothingness of the Void at its depths our home.

I can only imagine that when death finally greeted Quasimi, the reaper was met with infinite gratitude.

After his death, all of us who knew of the basin began to realize its reach and power. I suppose it was in the days following that my longing to be the basin's master seeded and grew.

When Flora hid the basin away, Isolt of the Waters languished.

I took full advantage of her lethargy. As my beloved queen slipped away, deeper and deeper into eternal slumber, I commandeered the basin.

At first, on her behalf ...

Now, I search for my own vessel of incarnation, writhing in anticipation as I anxiously await the perfect form.

For when we are united, we will ruin the Whole. And when the Whole is ruined, I will rule.

✧ ✧ ✧

"I come here often." Anton stood with Ryder in the room where Koldis was encased. "The sword is exquisite, is it not?" He ran his finger along the length of the glass, tracing the blade.

Now that he understood the source of its dark whispers, Ryder avoided staring at the malignant ruby in Koldis' hilt. Umbra sought a servant on the material plane to do his bidding. "Great beauty can mask grave danger."

"Perhaps—to those who are weak."

"Even the weak don't think of themselves that way," Ryder said.

"Such caution." Anton faced him. "I believe Umbra presents a unique opportunity in the evolution of the Whole."

"An opportunity to safeguard this sword and assure that Umbra remains in the Void."

"Let's go to my office," Anton's voice was strained.

Their walk through the library's main floor and across several courtyards was slow. Along the way, priest after priest wished to speak with Anton on some urgent matter. Ryder chafed as they sought to ingratiate themselves with the head of their Order. How could they be so blind to Anton's ambition and cruelty?

When they entered his office, Anton closed the door behind him. Ryder sat before Anton directed him to do so.

"I hear that your training with the guard was brief, as I suspected it would be." Anton ensconced himself in his new chair. It looked like a throne.

"I was injured in my first sparring match. I'll return to my classes with the guard physician's approval."

Anton's neck stiffened. "Did the sandstorm teach you nothing?"

"It taught me that I've earned the respect of the guard recruits."

Anton shook his head. "They don't need to respect you to serve you. You do realize that without the guard's help, your stubborn insistence upon saving your friends would have ended in the death of you."

The veins in Ryder's neck pulsed. "May I be excused?"

Anton's pale eyes bored into him. "No. I wish to discuss your studies with you."

Ryder sank deeper into his chair. Anton's idea of a discussion was to formulate his thoughts before a captive audience.

"I've given much thought these past years to Umbra. The entity amasses power with each passing day. Every time a mortal dies and doesn't pass into the Unknown Beyond, the entity assimilates the remnants of their energy. Imagine that power influenced by a strong and learned hand." He slid a single parchment across his desk.

Ryder read:

When the Dark Master rises from the mist to breach the veil, and a Daughter of Light, denied the throne by virtue of birth, stands alone, beware. Cunning will test the Grey Sentinel's shield.

If the Iron Bridge falls, and the Ancient Doors close, the end is near.

The blood of innocents will soak Illialei's meadows, and dreamlessness will snuff all hope from the mortal world. Fear not. This apocalyptic union can be saved. Though grace is undeserved, the purpose is love.

These are the mysteries yet untasted, on the tip of your tongue,
O Wayward Son of Idonne.—The Old Texts, Appendix VII

The poem disturbed Ryder, the way its flowery words enticed the butchery of war. He pushed the document back across the desk. "You believe this verse refers to Umbra's incarnation?"

"Yes, and more importantly, I believe it holds the key to confronting the power of the Albiana."

Every priest in the Order was assigned a separate sphere of knowledge. Prior to rising to head of the Order, Anton's area of expertise had been the Daughters of Light. Their mysterious governance of the Realm of Faerie, the enchanted world's most proximal country to the mortal world, provoked something within him akin to envy. Although Anton often questioned the Albiana queens' fitness to rule, the lineage's innate reserves of power fascinated him. His lectures upon the subject had always ended with a panel of questions: Should the seat of power in the enchanted world be shifted? Would it be better off in the hands of men? Did the knowledge and objectivity possessed by the Order of the Idonnai make them more suited to the task of governing?

Now, Ryder raised his eyes in question.

"Although the verse's author is anonymous, it's popularly known as the 'Idonnic Prophecy.' An odd fragment, the original version existed before Umbra formed," Anton explained. "It's included in the *Old Texts*, the only piece of writing within them that Olivia Albiana didn't pen herself. Of course, it's buried at the end of the work, included as a warning, not a vision of hope. It's what prompted my initial investigation into Umbra. "

"I'm not following you," Ryder said.

Anton waved his hand. Although generous with his opinions and theories about Illialei's queens, he was often secretive when it came to his research. "Before she took the throne, Olivia wrote a purposefully incomplete history of the Albiana lineage. A daughter's attempt to transform her mother's legacy, I suppose. She titled the work the *Old Texts* and ordered they be taught at the Bryndale schools, which she instated during her reign. Her daughter, Luisa, has continued the policy of educating a population which has no taste for books."

Ryder tried to keep up.

"Luisa's husband, Keir Collin, is a Huron. They have a daughter who will be the next queen. Although Luisa and Keir have never formally divorced, he returned to his homeland ages ago—the Albiana queens make poor wives, or so I'm told."

"And he is interested in Umbra's incarnation as well? As a way to deprive the Albiana—his daughter—of power?"

"If someone capable were to offer themselves to Umbra as the vessel of incarnation—"

"Someone such as yourself?"

"No. No. At my age, the risk would be far too great."

"Because?"

"The physiological impact alone would be unendurable. The optimal candidate would not only survive the incarnation, but swear allegiance to the Order."

"So you would harness Umbra's power?" Attempting diplomacy, Ryder added, "for the Order."

Anton inclined his head.

A band of tension squeezed Ryder's chest. Memories of Anton's bullying flashed through his mind. Umbra needed to be contained, not released on a plane where he could reek bloody carnage. Anton craved to wield that destructive power—in the name of some higher cause, perhaps. But he was a poor judge of higher causes. "My opinion aligns with Olivia Albiana," he said. "The verse is a warning. Perhaps a seduction, with its poetic allusion to love."

Anton surveyed his desk, his jaw rigid. Among the objects arrayed before him was a lion head rattle. His hand trembled as he grabbed its handle. "Without the basin, it's all speculation."

If Ryder could never escape the yoke of the priesthood, he would at least wear his robes with integrity. He wouldn't become a sycophant, or worse—Anton's pet. "Such tampering by the Order would circumvent the organic unfolding of the Whole."

Anton shook the ornamented toy. "Perhaps it was premature to have this conversation." He offered a cold smile. The last rays of sunlight, filtering through the window behind him, made the rattle's gem-embellished shell glitter as if it were enchanted.

Ryder's chest tightened. Whenever Anton toyed with that particular trinket, the young priest experienced an inexplicable urge to throttle his mentor. This evening was no different. Ryder gripped the edge of his chair. It gave the energy in his hands something to squeeze against.

Almost a year later, Ryder crouched at the seashore. One foot braced on a flat slab of rock, the other balanced upon a stony spindle. There was no port or ships on this isolated shoreline, only a flat horizon leading to infinity. More and more the young priest shirked his research to make the long hike to the Temple of

Delphinus. He'd discovered a rousing energy where the land met the sea. Wind gusts cleared his mind of every thought that was not his own, and amplified the whispers of his heart.

Ryder listened.

Here, at the edge of his familiar world, something called him. It brought a compelling urge to cross the Great White Sea, to sail to the Realm of Faerie. At first the young priest had accused his imagination, but the vapory insistence only become more inescapable, harder to push from his mind. It had scooped out a hollow in his chest. He would find no peace until he set foot upon the deck of a ship. Of itself that was not so troubling. But another impression followed in its wake. Although Anton had not yet returned to the subject of Umbra's incarnation, he'd shared more of the Albiana history with Ryder. The deeply disturbing stories increased the young priest's conviction that the power of Umbra must remain dormant, inaccessible to all who craved it.

If Ryder were to follow the intimations of his heart, if he were to leave Idonne, he must take Koldis with him.

The story continues in *Half Faerie*. Read the first chapter now.

The First Chapter of

Half Faerie

Defying the dark phase of the enchanted world's two moons, Melia imagined the light of a candle. A soft wind rustled the oak's leaves, and her timid inner flame snuffed out. She shifted on the tree's bough. "It's not going to work."

"Keep trying," Tatou encouraged her.

"It's hopeless."

Tatou's slight weight lifted from Melia's shoulder. A glowing orb in the pitch-black night, the pixie bobbed in front of her face. "Are you focusing on holding the flame steady?"

"Yes."

Tatou's natural radiance illuminated the half-faerie's slender hands and what was left of the ylandria clenched between her fingers. Melia held out her other hand. Tatou landed on the offered palm. "Are you relaxing?"

"How can I? Nothing is working." Melia's frustration bled into her voice. "Every thing I've tried to stop these stupid visions has failed." She smashed the ylandria butt against the tree limb before slipping the useless lump of faerie herb into her pocket. "One." She held up a finger. "Physical exhaustion. I ran across the fields until my legs gave out. Two." She raised a second finger. "A calming atmosphere. I buried myself in the meadows beneath morning glories and long grass—for an entire day! Three." She waved a third finger in the air. "Sleep deprivation. I forced myself to stay awake all three nights during the last dark moon phase."

Melia retrieved the burnt-out stub from her pocket and shook it in Tatou's face. "Now, this isn't working. What am I going to do?"

"Are there any seeds left?" Ylandria, a faerie herb whose vines wound through the tops of elm trees, was almost impossible to harvest. The pixie, eloquent in birdsong, had persuaded a swallow to gather the necessary volume for their experiment. She doubted she could do so again.

The half-faerie reached into her other pocket and fidgeted with the contents. "Yes, and another leaf."

"If you want to try again, I'll stay."

When Tatou had told Melia about the ylandria, and how it could help her control her inner eye, she couldn't wait to try it. Now, failure crushed her spirit. She couldn't even hold an imaginary flame steady.

Every second her desperation increased. What if she smoked more and it didn't make any difference? What if nothing ever made a difference? Why waste her friend's time?

"I don't want to make you later than you already are," Melia said.

Tatou was the only pixie who ever ventured beyond the enchanted gardens after midnight—and her late-night roaming made the other pixies wary of her. "A few more minutes won't matter."

"I'm sorry my mother stayed up so late." Pressina had returned to her study after dinner and lingered. "I wonder what she does down there," Melia mused, "in her room, carved out deep inside the oak's trunk."

"You know what she does ... black magic."

"But what kind of black magic?" Melia wondered out loud. "Other than Malachi, there's no evidence."

"Isn't he enough?"

"I suppose."

"Maybe you don't want to know what she's up to," Tatou said.

"You could be right about that," Melia huffed. But her mother's obsession with black magic aggravated her. "I'm just worried she's going to find out about these visions."

"How?"

"If Melusine or Plantine were to rummage through my mind while I'm having one, I'm sure they would tell her." The three sisters shared a telepathic connection.

Tatou puckered her lips with her fingers.

"Do you think they'd make me leave Illialei?" Melia asked.

"Who?"

"Whoever finds out"—Melia had given the subject a lot of thought—"my mother, or Queen Luisa, or a mob of flower faeries!"

"I've never heard of anyone being banished from Faerie before."

"Oh! And what about my father and every other mortal who broke a faerie troth?"

"That's different."

"I'm not so sure," Melia said. "What if they sent me back to the mortal world to live with him?" Her pulse quickened as her imagination leapt. She raised her palm higher to meet Tatou's gaze. "Or maybe they'd sentence me to death." Adopting a snooty tone, she mimicked, "Pressina bore it all in grim silence, a hard glint in her lilac eyes the only admission to the burden her middle child had always been."

Tatou giggled. "You sound like one of the flower faeries at the market."

Melia would have laughed at her own play-acting if she wasn't so afraid of what might happen if someone found out about the lifelike hallucinations of death and desolation that haunted her. She released a long, slow exhale.

"What?" Tatou asked.

"I was thinking about my thirteenth birthday."

"Why?"

Neither of them liked to talk about that day. Five years ago, after Queen Luisa's daughter, Lilliane, interrupted their celebration down by the river with a creepy joke about eating pixies, Tatou, Melia, and Plantine had trudged back to the tree house, their joy sapped. If that hadn't been enough to ruin the memory, Melia's father had telepathically interrogated her for the first time that night. He'd just discovered he shared the supersensory abilities his daughters possessed. None of them had been thrilled with the revelation. His attempts at telepathy were an invasion more than a conversation. Since then, during every dark-moon phase, gruesome images intruded into Melia's mind—gruesome images that she'd never seen or imagined before.

She knew it was all connected: her father's psychic trespass, the horrific visions, and the black nights when the enchanted world's two moons offered zero illumination.

"I had my first vision on the first night of the dark moon phase after that birthday," Melia said.

"What do you see, exactly?"

Melia's throat tightened. If her friend truly understood the images of slaughtered faeries and incinerated landscapes she saw —and the pleasure she took in witnessing them—she was sure Tatou would hate her or be frightened of her. She was frightened of herself, every time she experienced one. "It's better if I don't tell you." Tears welled in the half-faerie's eyes. She rubbed them away.

"What?" Tatou asked.

"When Melusine taught Plantine and me how to block Father's

telepathic intrusions, I became the best at building interior walls."
Sweat slicked Melia's palm. Tatou fluttered to the tree limb
nearest the half-faerie's head. "I was certain that would stop
everything."

"But it didn't," Tatou said.

"No."

"Do your sisters have them too?"

"No ... I don't know. I've never asked them." Melia's heart
hammered in her chest. "I don't think so. I mean, I've never
noticed them withdrawing the way I do." Or looking as guilty as
she felt. No matter how many psychic walls she threw up, or how
thick the walls were, when Faeries' moons went dark, the visions
came. The most logical explanation made her uneasy. They
weren't coming from outside her, they were bubbling up from
within.

"Try the ylandria one more time," Tatou said.

Melia fished the last leaf from her pocket. It was as hard to roll
the second time as the first, but this time its smoky haze seemed
more potent. She coughed on the peppery fumes. The last thing
she needed was to wake up her mother and sisters in the middle of
the night. She muffled the hacking sound with her free hand as her
eyes darted toward the tree house.

Everything remained quiet.

Relieved, Melia flicked ylandria ash into the engulfing darkness. When heat threatened her fingertips, she stubbed the glowing orange embers against the oak's branch and slipped the second butt into her pocket.

"What happened?" Tatou asked.

"The same thing. It flickered out."

"I'm sorry it didn't work. Are you going to be all right?"

"Sure. I'll see you tomorrow?"

"On the hill after school?"

Melia didn't remind her friend that she wouldn't be going to school tomorrow. She never went during the dark moon phase for fear of having a hallucination in class. The faeries and elves already kept their distance. How would they react if she fell into a trance right in front of them? "I'll be there."

The ball of Tatou's light shrank into a pinprick and then disappeared completely.

Melia slumped with her back bowing out, her elbows on her thighs, and her chin on the flats of her fists. They used to chase glow sprites on the shores of the Undine River, but now they experimented with faerie herbs. Maybe the ylandria wasn't working because she didn't want to know the truth. Her father's trespass had violated some inner boundary, one from which there was no retreat. It was a disturbing thought, to be forever transformed for the worse through no fault of her own, and at such an early age.

The ylandria's spicy fumes hung in the air. Melia sucked in a long breath. Her mind danced with energy. Focusing on a single flame seemed dull. She drew her knees up to rest her chin on them and turned her thoughts to her favorite fantasy. A pair of turquoise wings shimmered before her. Diamond chips laced the outer wings and lavender and emerald swirls patterned the inner wings. In her mind's eye, Melia reached out her hands and brushed an intricate mesh of downy feathers.

She dropped her legs, her feet swinging free, and gripped the branch she sat on with tight fingers. It helped her to connect the muscle and bone of her torso and shoulders with the wings in her mind's eye. With a gentle flutter, a slow flap, and a coordinated beating, she shot upwards. Delighted with her mental creation, she soared higher than any faerie of flower or field ever could.

The enormous oak cradling the tree house shrank below. She faced east, toward the meadows, but she wanted to fly toward the sea. She prepared to make the wide arc west—and froze. A familiar force wrested control of her mind. It erupted from deep within her

213

and superimposed an alternate reality.

I sniff the air. Something burns. I search the skyline for smoke. Heat and cinders explode beneath me.

I land on the ground. Sparks snap in the night. The tree house crackles. Flames run up its walls and prance across the roof. Bright tongues lick the towering oak. A wall of heat blisters my skin and scorches a trail to the Sylvan Forest. Heart-wrenching screeches explode in the night. I cover my ears. An enormous buck tramples the blaze, leading a stampede of deer. Following on their trail, an army of smaller woodland animals scurry from the inferno.

One of the oak's branches split, the tree house lurches.

Mother screams.

I can't see my father, yet from some hidden recess he encourages me, "Let it run wild."

I throw back my head and laugh.

"Wake up." Her mother squeezed her shoulder, pinching her skin.

Melia twisted free of the grip. She was on the ground. Flat on her back. Everything throbbed. She must have fallen out of the tree.

"It's the middle of the night. What are you doing out here?" her mother asked.

Melia felt more than saw Pressina lean over her. She jabbed her heels in the dirt, pushing her body away. The ylandria had tasted sharp, not unpleasant. Could her mother smell its distinctive fragrance in her hair? Or on her nightgown? She couldn't tell. To Melia, the burning maelstrom of her vision still lingered. She wiped her nose with the back of her hand, hoping to clear the smell of charred wood.

"Do I smell ylandria?"

Melia rolled farther away and stood up. A twig poked through her nightgown. She brushed it, along with some leaves and grass, from her back. Her side felt tender, but nothing worse. She'd probably have some bruises in the morning.

"Answer me."

Honesty was useless. "I couldn't sleep."

Before she could dodge Pressina's hand, her mother's long fingers dug the two ylandria butts from the pocket in Melia's nightgown.

How had she managed that? Melia could barely distinguish her mother's shape—the slightest shade darker than the night around her.

Pressina grabbed her daughter's arm and pulled her toward the spiral steps circling the oak.

Resistance would only fuel her anger.

In the front room, Melusine and Plantine huddled together on their mother's favorite lime-striped chaise. They each held a candle. Otherwise the room was dark. Malachi, Mother's botched spell of a cat, hissed from the shadows as her mother dragged Melia into the kitchen.

"Melusine, Plantine, bring the candles," their mother commanded.

Her sisters pressed their melting sticks into the holders on the table. Melia formed a barrier over her chest with her arms. The flickering light drove home her failure; the ylandria had increased the power of her visions, not her control over them. While she'd dreamed of wings and flight, her timid inner flame—the one that had kept blowing out—ignited an inner inferno in some back corridor of her mind. She reached out to one of the kitchen chairs to steady herself.

Melusine's blue eyes burned with suspicion. Plantine's pained gaze was the one she always wore when Melia got in trouble.

"You were laughing hysterically," Pressina said. "It was so loud, you woke us up."

"Sorry I interrupted your beauty sleep."

"It was an evil laugh," Melusine said.

"All right, off to bed," their mother dismissed Melusine and Plantine. Neither dared challenge her, a testament to her angry state. Pressina pulled out a chair and eased into it.

Melia didn't move.

"What were you doing smoking ylandria?"

For a split second, Melia considered whether her mother might help. But Pressina resented the telepathic connection her daughters shared with their father. Bringing it up would infuriate her.

The color of her mother's lilac eyes deepened. "Where did you get it?"

Melia made a meal out of one of her fingernails. She'd be fending off her mother's glamour soon.

Pressina threw the butts on the table. Her ivory wings quivered.

Melia should have had an equally striking pair. But no, the Whole had played a cruel joke. As a half-faerie, she lived with a psychic bond to her mortal father—which she didn't want—and as a

half-mortal, she lived without the one thing that she yearned for—
which her faerie mother had—wings.

The shade of Pressina's eyes reached purple-black. A tendril of
her will, an invisible leash, made her daughter's lip quiver with a
desire to confess.

Furious, Melia dropped her gaze. It wasn't enough that her
father's psychic probing had opened a doorway in her mind she
needed to close, now her mother was trying to glamour her. She
wasn't going to let her. Not tonight, not ever again.

Melia shifted her focus to the wax pearling down the sides of the
candles. "I just wanted to try it."

"What am I going to do with you?"

"Send m-me to b-bed without sup-supper?"

The silly comment snapped her mother's concentration.

Melia tipped her head ever so slightly, to confirm the glamour
had failed, but it was hardly a triumph.

Now, Pressina's eyes blazed with dissatisfaction. Faeries—
always charming and graceful—didn't stutter. Her mother didn't
need to say the words out loud. Pressina's harsh thoughts seeped
beneath her daughter's skin: You're an abomination.

Melia gulped.

Pressina swept the ylandria butts into her palm, closed her hand into a fist, and jiggled them for emphasis. "The herbs in Illialei are potent, even to full-blooded faeries. Ylandria is toxic to mortals in large doses. When you decided to smoke this stuff, did you ever stop to think you're only half faerie?"

"How could I forget?" Melia pushed the words through clenched teeth.

"Stop feeling sorry for yourself. You don't know the half of it."

"Then tell me."

Her mother waved her hand, indicating there wouldn't be any telling tonight. Not surprising, Pressina forever hinted at a trunk-load of secrets she was either too afraid or too noble to reveal.

"If you're going to experiment with faerie herbs, get some reliable information."

Melia swallowed the challenge she wanted to make about reliable information. Her mother was winding down, no need to wind her back up again.

"Sh-sure."

"If you're not careful, you'll end up as wasted as one of those pathetic full-blooded mortals who comes to Faerie and loses their way forever."

"A pathetic, full-blooded mortal like my father?"

"We're done here," Pressina said.

Finally.

Melia stomped down the hall. She wished she could stomp right out of the tree house and into another life.

The next morning, Melia feigned a headache. After she heard Plantine's steps on the oak's spiral staircase, she rolled over and waited for Melusine's slippered feet to patter by. The nest of blue jays who made their home in the oak chattered outside her window. Melia tiptoed over to say, "Good morning," to them. She caught sight of Melusine headed toward the river, probably off to the mortal world with her faerie friends.

Her mother's bedroom door creaked open. Melia dove back beneath the covers. If she was quiet, Pressina wouldn't notice her middle daughter was skipping school–again. Not that her mother cared. She was always distracted these days, disappearing into her subterranean room to study magic, or whatever else she did down there.

Melia didn't want to answer questions about ylandria–or anything else–this morning. She cracked her bedroom door open. When she heard the lock click on the door of her mother's study, Melia's body relaxed. Now, she just had to get out of the tree house and stay gone for the rest of the day. She ran her fingers through her long, dark hair as she tried to decide what to wear. A worn summer coat and several sleeveless dresses filled her closet. She reached for the orange one. As she pulled it over her head, she half-listened for her mother. The tree house remained quiet.

Barefoot, Melia padded down the hall.

The great oak's columnar trunk formed the central pillar of the tree house. From its axis, a single layer of branches spanned the front room, wheel-like, about two feet beneath the high ceiling. From his high perch on one of the limbs, Malachi fixed his strange golden eyes on Melia. When she passed underneath him, he hissed. Melia walked backward with curled fingers, taunting the odd creature as he continued to glower at her.

When he started to yowl, she spun and scooted out the door, running with light feet on the oak's steps. No doubt his annoying whines would draw Pressina from her study—they were about the only thing that did.

On the bottom stair, Melia's stomach growled. She headed in the direction opposite Melusine had gone, toward Bryndale.

A little while later, she wandered through the city's vegetable market.

The other shoppers stared more than usual as she sauntered by.

Yes, I should be in school. No, I'm not there. She stopped at the tomato stand to pick up a couple of Marguerite's famous beefsteaks.

"It was one of Pressina's daughters."

When she overheard her mother's name, Melia froze.

"She was *howling* outside the tree house."

A lump formed in the half-faerie's throat. Two old elves—she could tell by their thick, nasal voices—gossiped on the other side of the canvas wall in the stall that sold broccoli and cauliflower.

"If you ask me, it has everything to do with him. After all these years, he's still obsessed with Pressina."

The voices softened. Melia grabbed two ripe fruits and shoved past a group of field faeries. She pressed her ear against the divider to see if she could hear anything else.

"How long has it been? A decade? Almost two?"

"Longer than that in the mortal world."

"They say he's discovered a way to incarnate Umbra."

"Why does he want to stir up that kind of trouble?"

"He thinks it will change the laws between the worlds."

"So?"

"The old laws keep him out of Faerie, maybe the new laws will let him back in."

"Mortals!" The first elf's condescension rang out loud and clear. "What part of breaking a faerie troth does he not understand? You don't get a second chance. That's the point. He needs to move on. Forget about Pressina and incarnating Umbra."

"Are you going to tell him?"

"And miss my afternoon nap, when I've got dibs on the shadiest spot in the glen?"

Snort. "Have you seen the girls?"

"Pretty enough, but they don't have any wings."

"I heard the one involved in the incident last night is dangerous."

"They don't belong here. Pressina should have left them in the mortal world with him."

The elves wandered off.

Melia's impulse to rip aside the curtain and rain ripe tomatoes down upon the mouthy pair came too late. Red-orange juice oozed over her hands. Seeds and pulp splattered her dress. She'd squeezed the tomatoes so hard they burst.

A few feet away, a couple of flower faeries whispered.

"What are you looking at?" she demanded.

They tittered and preened, flaring their wings.

Melia stalked away.

He was the great mortal druid, Elynus—her father. Apparently, sowing her visions wasn't enough. Now, he was going to incarnate Umbra, whatever that meant.

Melia's jaw tightened as she hiked out of town.

Stupid elves. She was *laughing,* not howling.

Author's Note

I've hoped to publish the stories included in this prequel for many years. Back in 2007, when I began to imagine the Whole, these tales were key to its development. My experience in life has proven that great shifts in individual consciousness ride the long tail of collective historic events. Thus one of the series themes: The gaining of consciousness is a lengthy process that spans generations.

Another theme in the series is the spiritual impact of a mother on her child. I'm talking about the non- or pre- verbal communication that occurs in the womb. A gift the child carries through their lifetime, a gift the child may or may not choose to mine.

Due to the many kinds of limitations inherent in being human, the dreams we dream can be excruciatingly challenging to manifest. It doesn't mean we shouldn't dream them. It means the world, the universe, life itself, benefits from every tiny step we take in the evolution of our species.

My mother and my maternal grandmother were labeled crazy and eccentric, respectively. I could not have loved two women more. Writing *Daughter of Light* is my effort to thank them for the intangible things they gave me that have enriched my life, as much as it is a way to encourage all daughters to live in the light of the women who have loved them.

Sincerely,
Heidi

Thank You

I appreciate you spending your valuable time reading *Isolt's Enchantment*. If you'd like to share the story with other readers, please tell a friend, or post a review on any book-ish site.

I'd also like to invite you to sign up for my newsletter: http://eepurl.com/wWKUj. It's quirky—like me:D—and I confess, it comes out sporadically, but I send a variety of things, including some (hopefully) pleasant surprises along with updates on all my new releases.

Sincerely,

Acknowledgments

Many thanks to:

Sheila, for early reading and valuable feedback

Vince, for pushing me beyond my edges

About the Author

Heidi Garrett is the author of the *Daughter of Light* fantasy trilogy about a young half-faerie, half-mortal searching for her place in the Whole.

She's also the author of *Once Upon a Time Today*, a collection of modern fairy tale retellings for adults who have already left home. *The Magic Cupcake* series is paranormal romance she writes with Billie Limpin.

Heidi was born in Texas, and attempted to reside in as many cities in that state as possible. She made it to Houston, Lubbock, Austin, and El Paso. After spending a decade in southern California, she now lives in Eastern Washington state with her husband, their two cats, her laptop, and her Kindle. Being from the South, she often contemplates the magic of snow.

Heidi Garrett

You can find Heidi on her blog.

Glossary of Characters and Creatures

The Albiana: Although they are of unknown origin, the Albianas are considered flower faeries. However, they are taller than most flower faeries, and their alabaster skin remains pale even when exposed to sunlight. They are the most beautiful of all the faeries.

Basil: The Grand Library's ginger tabby cat.

Brownies: Ruddy-faced, dark-haired, playful creatures, they usually stand about three feet high. Some choose to serve in the Cathedral Palace Guard.

Aldous: A wood elf, he is the head librarian of the Cathedral

Palace Grand Library.

Anton: An Idonnai, Ryder's mentor, and the head of the Order of the Idonnai.

Ava Albiana: The second queen of Illialei, she was Gwyneth Albiana's daughter.

Captain Tom: Captain of the Lucky Seahorse.

Cult of Umbra: An army of muannai who will serve the incarnated Umbra.

Dwarves: Dwarves originally populated the planet Una in the mortal world. However, when Isolt of the Waters, an ancient water elemental, was banished from Una by her husband, the god Vulcan, the dwarves abandoned Una with her. Una became known as Earth, and the dwarves migrated from Earth to Misgradde by way of the Realm of Faerie. A sizable population of dwarves never made it to Misgradde. They remained in Tyrannis as chefs when it was discovered their talent for cooking was as great as their talent for metalwork.

Elendah, the Grey Faerie of Aldaine: The only grey faerie who does not dwell on the Isle of Minnanon, Elendah sits on the throne of the Stronghold of Calashai in Tyrannis. She is known as the regent of the stronghold.

Elynus: The Great Mortal Druid. Estranged husband to

Pressina. Father to Melia, Melusine, and Plantine. Exiled to the mortal world.

Evangeline: A mermaid Melia meets in the mortal world.

Field Faeries: The faeries related to non-blooming plants. Typically, their physical appearance is plainer than that of the flower faeries. They have wings and are capable of short flights at low altitude. Average height is five feet.

Flora: The sole surviving spring faerie in the Whole.

Flower Faeries: The faeries related to blooming plants. Typically, the females are of great beauty. They have wings and are capable of short flight at low altitudes. Average height is five feet. Verbena, Clementine, Brigitta, Giselle, and Marguerite are flower faeries.

Garrick: An Idonnai and baker, husband to Shilda. He is like a father to Ryder.

Glow Sprites, Nixies, and Undines: The water creatures native to Tyrannis. They live in the Undine River.

Gnomes: Stand about two feet high and wear red hats. Native to the Ruadain in northern Tyrannis, they are taciturn creatures and not friendly.

The Grey Council: Composed of grey faeries and located on the Isle of Minnanon, it is the supreme ruling body in the enchanted world.

Grey Faeries: Wise and ageless, a small population dwell on the Isle of Minnanon in the enchanted world.

Gumf: A dwarf, the proprietor of the Veiled Tavern in the Balyudor in Tyrannis.

Gweff: The dwarf who forged the magical basin, Ormrun.

Gwyneth Albiana: From unknown origins, she was Illialei's first queen.

Haff: The dwarf who forged the magical sword, Koldis.

Huron Knights: The fair-haired natives of Huros. Considered to be the most chivalrous inhabitants in the enchanted world.

Isolt of the Waters: An ancient water elemental banished to the Void by her husband, the god Vulcan.

Lilliane Albiana: Illialei's faerie princess and daughter of Queen Luisa Albiana.

Luisa Albiana: The reigning queen of Illialei.

Malachi: A cat-like creature. The result of one of Pressina's botched spells.

Melia: A half-faerie. The middle daughter of the mortal druid Elynus and the full-blooded faerie Pressina. She has no wings.

Melusine: A half-faerie. The oldest daughter of the mortal druid Elynus and the full-blooded faerie Pressina. She has no wings. Melusine's story was legend in 15th century France.

Mermaids: The water creatures native to Illialei. They enjoy traveling to the mortal world.

Moog: A troll, he serves Lord Zachariah Goring. He transports communications between the mortal and enchanted worlds for the mortal druid Elynus.

Morgannai: A warrior race, they are the dark-haired natives of Morganna.

The Muannai (singular muannaye): Tall (over five feet) and lean, they are the wingless dark faeries native to Tyrannis. They are the only creatures in the enchanted world who cannot travel to the mortal world.

Nandana: A mortal, also known as the Illustrator, she lives in Illialei. Her body art is popular among the faeries and elves.

Ogres: Huge creatures from Kyrakkos. They are strong, but simple-minded and slow. Often described as smelling of mold.

Olivia Albiana: The fourth queen of Illialei, she was Uriel's daughter. She is Queen Luisa's mother.

The Order of the Idonnai: An order of priests in Idonne. They chronicle and observe events in the Whole. However, they do not intervene.

Pixies: The most petite faeries. They are approximately four to six inches tall and dwell in the enchanted gardens. Known to be mischievous.

Plantine: A half-faerie. The youngest daughter of the mortal druid Elynus and the full-blooded faerie Pressina. She has no wings.

Pogo: A troll and Moog's twin brother. He has served Sevondi's lineage for centuries.

Pressina: A full-blooded faerie. Estranged wife to Elynus. Maintains a private life in Illialei with her three daughters: Melia, Melusine, and Plantine. She studies and practices black magic.

Ryder: A young priest fleeing his duties as a member of the Order of the Idonnai. An orphan, he was abandoned at the priesthood's gates as an infant.

Sevondi: A dragonwitch. She is a muannaye. Her great-great-grandfather was a sorcerer from Kyrakkos.

Shilda: An Idonnai and skilled herbalist, wife to Garrick. She is like a mother to Ryder.

Sinjiin: A mage from the Hidden City.

Spring Faeries: A race of warrior faeries native to Illialei.

Tatou: A pixie. She is Melia's best friend.

Tree Elves: Thinner and taller than wood elves, they are native to eastern Illialei.

Trolls: Both the males and females of the species stand about three feet tall. However, the males tend to be balding, with swarthy skin and large noses, while the females—though often stout—have thick, luxurious hair, bewitching eyes, and cherubic faces.

Tuck: A tree elf, he is Aldous' apprentice at the Cathedral Palace Grand Library.

Typhons: Natives of Typhos, considered to be the enchanted world's best sailors.

Umbra: A non-corporeal entity dwelling in the Void. He is a growing mass of mortal psychic ash, a result of rapid population growth in the mortal world. Umbra has developed a discrete identity and seeks to incarnate in the material plane. He requires a living material person/creature as a vessel for his consciousness. He seeks to ruin and rule the Whole.

Uriel Albiana: The third queen of Illialei, she was Ava Albiana's daughter.

Wood Elves: Mostly rather round, they stand about four feet tall and are native to western Illialei.

Zachariah Goring, Lord: A muannaye, he collaborated with the mortal druid Elynus to incarnate Umbra.

Glossary of Places and Things

Achill Island: An island in the country of Ireland in the mortal world. Birthplace of Elynus and Pressina's daughters: Melia, Melusine, and Plantine.

Achill Head: The most westerly point of Achill Island.

Aldaine: A city in Tyrannis located on the highest, north most peak of the Ruadain Mountains in the enchanted world.

Ashleam Bay: The western coast of Achill Island.

Azyllai: A country in the enchanted world. Home to the gods.

The Balyudor: The wild woods in Tyrannis.

Bryndale: The largest city in Illialei.

The Cathedral Palace: The primary palace in Illialei. Gwyneth Albiana's husband, a lesser god, built the palace for her. She ascended the Cathedral Palace throne as the first queen of Illialei.

The Cimmerian Inlet: An inlet to the Great White Sea, located in northern Tyrannis, in proximity to the Stronghold of Calashai.

The Crossroads: A popular tavern in the seaport of Typhos.

The Danu Meadows: A large meadow in central Illialei.

The Enchanted Gardens: Home of the pixies. The gardens border the Sylvan Forest in western Illialei.

The Enchanted World: Known territories include: The Realm of Faerie, the Great White Sea, Idonne, Morganna, Typhos, Huros, Kyrakkos, Azyllai, the Isle of Minnanon, and Misgradde.

The Flower of Isbelline: A striking flower with creamy white petals that blooms on the northern most sea cliffs of the Ruadain Mountains.

The Footing Fields: The fields of Illialei where brownies roll ball and play other games.

The Glen: A wooded valley that lies between the Rolling Mountains and the Nyssalei in western Illialei. Home to the largest population of wood elves in Illialei.

The Grand Library: The library in the Cathedral Palace.

The Great White Sea: The largest body of water in the enchanted world. Reputed to have mystical and healing properties.

The Hidden City: Home to the most powerful mages in the enchanted world. Its location is hidden from all who do not dwell there.

High Hill: A large hill in Illialei.

The Hive: A cafe in Bryndale that caters to wood elves. Honey is an ingredient in all the items on the menu.

Huros: Home of the fair-haired Hurons. Huron Knights are considered to be the most chivalrous in the enchanted world.

Illialei: One of two countries comprising the Realm of Faerie. In older days, it was known as the Territory of Light. It is considered the heart of the enchanted world.

Idonne: Home to the priesthood of the Idonnai. Idonnai, who are not members of the priesthood, are considered to be the finest artisans in the enchanted world.

The Idonnic Library: The priesthood of the Idonnai's work and purpose for existence. Its pristine architecture is the seat of Idonnic power and influence in the enchanted world.

The Isle of Minnanon: An isolated island in the northern waters of the Great White Sea. The Grey Council and the largest surviving population of grey faeries reside on the Isle.

Koldis: The dwarf, Haff, forged the magical sword in the bowels of the Ruadain Mountains.

Kyrakkos: Considered the font of black magic, it is home to the most powerful sorcerers and witches in the enchanted world.

Lake Vivientiana: A lake in eastern Illialei.

The Maeldun Bridge: The iron bridge that crosses the Nyssalei River between Illialei and Tyrannis. It is an in-between place.

Mare Cliffs: (pronounced mah-**ray**) The high cliffs that follow the Nyssalei River as it runs through eastern Illialei. Sylphs from Tyrannis have been known to cross into Illialei to dive from the cliffs into the river.

Misgradde: The country with the largest population of dwarves in the enchanted world.

Morganna: Home to the dark-haired Morgannai. The Morgannai are the enchanted world's warrior race.

The Mortal World: Home to mortals. Although it is not part of the enchanted world, the mortal world and the enchanted world must sustain a dynamic equilibrium of metaphysical energies for the Whole to function optimally.

The Muannai Valley: Borders the Undine River in southeast Tyrannis. Home to the largest population of muannai. Where the Muannai Valley Marketplace is located.

The Muannai Valley Marketplace: A large market in the muannai valley.

The Nuada: The plains of central Tyrannis.

The Nyssalei River: The river that borders and runs through Illialei. It runs from Lake Vivientiana into the Great White Sea.

Ormrun: The dwarf, Gweff, forged the bejeweled basin in the bowels of the Ruadain Mountains to be used as a portal by Isolt of the Waters.

The Parallel of Shadows: The shadowy realm between the Void and the enchanted world.

Pebble Rock: A large boulder with a natural cleft comfortable for sitting. It marks the head of the most popular trail through the Sylvan Forest.

The Primal Essence: Where all life—mortal and enchanted—begins.

The Realm of Faerie: A single land mass in the enchanted world comprised of two countries, Illialei and Tyrannis. The Realm of Faerie is the only country in the enchanted world that shares contiguous borders of time and space with the mortal world.

The Rolling Mountains: A hilly mountain range spanning eastern and western Illialei.

The Ruadain Mountains: A seven peak mountain range in northern Tyrannis.

The Sapphire Lily: The flower that grew from the seed Gwyneth Albiana planted on the shores of Lake Vivientiana when she first arrived in Illialei.

Southend: Illialei's port.

The Stronghold of Calashai: The four-towered stronghold in the center of Aldaine. Elendah, the Grey Faerie of Aldaine, sits on the stronghold's throne as regent.

The Summer Palace: A smaller palace in Illialei, located on the shores of Lake Vivientiana.

The Sylvan Forest: A light-filled forest located in northwest Illialei.

Typhos: Home to the Typhons and the enchanted world's largest and busiest seaport, Maris. Typhons are considered to be the best sailors in the enchanted world.

Tyrannis: One of the two countries comprising the Realm of Faerie. In older days, it was known as the Dark Lands.

The Undine River: Branches from a fork in the Nyssalei River and flows through Tyrannis.

The Unknown Beyond: A place beyond the Whole, about which little is known.

The Veiled Tavern: A mystical inn located in the heart of the Balyudor. Gumf, a dwarf and devout epicurean, is the inn's proprietor. He employs a large number of dwarves at the tavern as they are reputed to be the best chefs in the Whole.

The Void: The realm of incorporeal existence.

The Whole: Includes: The mortal world, the enchanted world, the Void, the Parallel of Shadows, and the Primal Essence. (The Unknown Beyond is not part of the Whole.)

www.ingramcontent.com/pod-product-compliance
Lightning Source LLC
Chambersburg PA
CBHW022157170626
46807CB00005B/2243